E.R.

Blood pressure is high and pulses are racing
in these fast-paced, dramatic stories from
Mills & Boon® Medical Romance™.
They'll move a mountain to save a life
in an emergency, be they E.R. doctors, nurses or
paramedics. There are lots of critical engagements
amongst the high tensions and emotional passions
in these exciting stories of lives and loves at risk!

Dear Reader,

I love a good wedding—romance in the air, dressed in your best and looking as close to a million dollars as you're ever likely to get. The perfect place to meet the man of you dreams, really.

But what happens when the shine wears off along with the lip gloss? What happens when one night of heavy flirting ties you to someone in ways you could never have anticipated? How do you cope when the man of your dreams suddenly becomes your landlord and boss to boot?

That was the setting I created for my gorgeous heroine Leah and my sexy hero Cole. Between them they created a lot of laughs and a lot of tears, and hopefully a love story you'll enjoy reading as much as I enjoyed writing!

Happy reading,

Carol Marinelli

The Consultant's Accidental Bride

Carol Marinelli

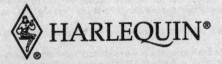

HARLEQUIN®

TORONTO • NEW YORK • LONDON
AMSTERDAM • PARIS • SYDNEY • HAMBURG
STOCKHOLM • ATHENS • TOKYO • MILAN • MADRID
PRAGUE • WARSAW • BUDAPEST • AUCKLAND

ISBN 0-373-06471-3

THE CONSULTANT'S ACCIDENTAL BRIDE

First North American Publication 2004

www.eHarlequin.com

Printed in U.S.A.

PROLOGUE

'I HAVE to get this flight!' Struggling to keep the note of desperation out of her voice, Leah took a deep breath, knowing that losing her temper wasn't going to get her anywhere. 'I know how stupid I must look—I mean I've seen those airline shows, where people argue at the desk, when everyone knows that they haven't got a leg to stand on—but it really is imperative that I get that flight.'

'Then you should have confirmed your seat, Miss Jacobs,' came the unimpressed response.

'It's Leah,' she said through gritted teeth. 'I thought we'd at least be on first-name terms by now, Glynn.'

Glynn flashed her a very false smile. 'Then you should have confirmed, *Leah*.'

It was like a broken record. They'd been arguing the point for half an hour now. Leah could see on the overhead screen that the final calls were being made and though she knew that her tears were wasted here, that feminine wiles weren't going to win over this guy in particular, the sparkle of tears in her eyes as she again pleaded her case were far from staged.

'As I've said, economy's full…'

'Then upgrade me?' she pleaded hopefully.

'I'm sorry I just don't have that kind of authority. Anyway, Business Class is practically full with a load

5

of doctors returning to Melbourne from a medical conference we've had here in Cairns.'

'So there are some seats?' The hope that flared in her voice died even before she'd completed her sentence as Glynn's eyes dragged over her, and Leah could feel him snootily taking in the scraggy blonde curls tied back in a scrunchy, the faded denim shorts and scanty T-shirt that had definitely seen better days, all topped off with a rather sad-looking backpack. No doubt, Leah thought, cringing with mortification under his scrutiny, he was probably realising why he'd chosen to pursue his own type in the first place.

'My best friend gets married tomorrow,' Leah begged. 'I'm the bridesmaid.'

'So you said,' Glynn replied tightly. 'And, as I've pointed out, with your type of ticket, seventy-two hours' confirmation prior to flying is obligatory.' His botoxed forehead almost creased in exasperation as Leah attempted to break in, but Glynn got there first. 'I know you're flying to the UK on Sunday,' he said through gritted teeth, holding up a very manicured hand to silence her as he did so. 'And I know that there isn't anywhere you can possibly stay tonight, given that all your friends are either back in England or have moved on to Brisbane. I know that because you've already told me—several times,' he added. 'But, as I've explained, the best I can offer is a flight to Melbourne at ten a.m. tomorrow. Now, if you'll take a seat I'll see if I can arrange some meal vouchers for you.'

'I don't want—'

'Sorry I didn't confirm.' A voice that didn't sound

remotely sorry came rather loudly from the next checkin desk and both Leah and Glynn turned, a temporary standoff ensuing as for a moment or two their attention was diverted as they gaped in admiration at the gentleman at the next desk.

Drop-dead gorgeous just about summed him up. Very black hair, coiled over a white shirt, and heavily lidded navy eyes flashed a winning smile as he rummaged through his suit pocket for his ticket. 'I thought the hotel had taken care of all that.'

'No problem, Dr Richardson,' the pretty ground staff assistant gushed. 'They're boarding now at Gate Four. I'll just ring through and let them know that you're on your way.'

At least Glynn had the grace to blush.

'Look.' Glynn's smile even bordered on sympathetic as he turned his attention back to Leah. 'Given that it was a genuine misunderstanding, I'll see if the airline can arrange some accommodation. I can't make any promises, I'll have to talk to my supervisor first. I'm sorry, Leah, it's the best I can do.'

His hand was outstretched, as it had been for the best part of the entire conversation, holding out her tickets in the hope she would just give in and take them, and this time she did.

It was pointless getting angry with Glynn, Leah reasoned, he was just doing his job.

Sitting on one of the endless empty seats, Leah cast her eyes around the deserted airport. She'd always assumed that airports were constantly buzzing, a perpetual flow of people forever milling through. After all, it had been packed when she'd first arrived, just like a mini-Heathrow really with monitors reeling off arrivals and departures and frazzled parents attempting to control even more frazzled toddlers. But, unlike the twenty-four seven circus of Heathrow, the day was obviously over here. The car hire place had pulled down its shutters, the café was in darkness. Only the piped music broke the silence, and Leah stared blankly at a massive array of greenery lining the windows, which was so lush it was hard to tell where the indoor plants ended and the outside began. A couple of cleaners were half-heartedly running their dust mops along the highly polished floors and for a tiny moment it reminded Leah of her own emergency room back in England at four a.m. But there was no nostalgia as her mind wandered back to her workplace, no fond memories trickling or eagerness to get back to where she belonged. Instead, a bubble of panic welled inside…

Oh, it was all very well to blame Glynn, all very well to point the finger and insist she truly hadn't known it was necessary to confirm her flight, but what would be the point?

Burying her head in her hands, Leah let out a low moan. Never in a million years would she deliberately have hurt Kathy. Never in a million years would she have wanted to miss her best friend's wedding, but when they had arranged it, when Kathy had first told her of her plans, a year had seemed such a long way off.

The wedding of the century, Kathy marrying her delicious Australian and heading back to London for a prolonged honeymoon, with Leah just a day behind.

The perfect end to the perfect year.

And what a year, Leah thought with a fond smile. She'd climbed Ayer's Rock, snorkelled her way along the Barrier Reef, swum with dolphins and packed so many memories into twelve months it was almost impossible to fathom. But all good things must come to an end, Leah thought sadly. This time next week she'd be back in Emergency, this time next week she'd be pulling on her uniform and picking up where she'd left off, and the thought truly terrified her.

She didn't want to go back.

Maybe missing the flight had been some sort of unintentional Freudian slip, maybe it hadn't been entirely an accident.

'Miss Jacobs?'

Looking up, Leah hastily wiped a stray tear, determined to apologise for giving Glynn such a hard time. A hotel and free meal sounded just about the order of the day.

'I've spoken to my supervisor and, given the fact you've only got hand luggage...' Holding out his hand, he gave her what looked suspiciously like a boarding card, imparting his first genuine smile as Leah stared at him blankly 'If you run you should just make it. The plane's departing from Gate Four.'

'I was just getting used to the idea that I'd missed it,' Leah admitted. 'Would it be terribly bad if I told you I'd changed my mind?'

Glynn laughed, actually laughed. 'I knew there was a reason I swore off women.' This time his smile really was sympathetic. 'Having second thoughts about going home, huh?'

Leah nodded. 'And third and fourth.'

'Would it help if I told you you're flying business class?'

Blinking at the boarding card, a smile inched over her face.

'And that that gorgeous specimen of a man that checked in a few minutes ago will be sitting in the next seat?'

'Possibly.' Leah grinned, picking up her backpack and slinging it over her shoulders, and even though it was probably way down on Glynn's list of must haves he got it anyway.

Leaning over, she kissed his smooth tanned cheek.

'Thanks, Glynn.'

'Send me a postcard!'

Running along the empty corridor, dodging the occasional buggy loaded with domestics, she just made it. Pushing her boarding card through the machine, Leah ran down the carpeted aisle, ignoring the pursed lips of the cabin crew as she handed over her card.

'To the left, third row from the front.'

Finally!

Finally she'd see what went on behind those smart navy curtains that were pulled as the plane taxied along the runway, finally she'd find out if the chairs really did go all the way back and if the drinks really were free!

Biting on her lip as an air steward relieved her of her backpack, Leah took a deep breath and slipped into her seat.

OK, it was only the first leg of the journey, but finally she was on her way home.

CHAPTER ONE

'YOU made it, then?'

Slipping into her seat, Leah let out a long, exaggerated sigh before turning to her travelling companion. Glynn hadn't been exaggerating. He really was heavenly. Superbly cut straight black hair, smoothed back from his tanned face, those stunning navy eyes, smiling as he looked over. To say he was well groomed would be an overwhelming understatement. He'd discarded his jacket, but his cotton shirt was still crisp, and his tie, though loosened, certainly hadn't been thrown on and Leah felt like a charity advertisement in comparison.

'I thought I'd missed it,' Leah admitted. 'I really thought the plane was leaving without me. I can't believe they actually let me on.'

'It must be because you travel light.'

Leah laughed. 'That's a first! Normally I need a tow truck for my backpack, but I sent a massive parcel home by sea mail yesterday, otherwise I'd undoubtedly have been on the next flight and paying excess baggage to boot.'

'Cole Richardson.' Even his hand was immaculate, Leah thought, beautifully manicured, the glint of a heavy gold watch under a crisp white cuff. But extremely disappointingly, Leah realised as she held out her rather scrawny nail-bitten offering, was the heavy gold band on his ring finger.

'Leah Jacobs.' She smiled, mentally scolding herself. As if a guy as effortlessly divine as Cole wouldn't be taken. Not that she was on the lookout for romance, it was just the mental checklist every half-respectable single girl did when they met a halfway decent man for the first time. Despite her internal sigh, the fact he was wearing a wedding ring actually helped. There was nothing worse than, a few hours in, finding out that the man you'd actually started to like had a wife and nine children at home or even an LSG, as Kathy and she had abbreviated longstanding girlfriend to.

Or in Glynn's case, a significant other.

No, far better to know from the outset that this was one tree it definitely wasn't worth barking up.

'From your accent, I take it you're from England.' When she nodded he carried on, 'So how long have you been in Australia?'

'A year,' Leah answered. 'I'm heading back on Sunday. How about you? Are you on your way home?'

Cole nodded. 'I've been at a medical conference in Cairns.'

'Ah, yes.' Leah grinned. '*Dr* Richardson. And from what I remember, you didn't confirm your flight either.'

She was sure they would have carried on talking but the plane, which had been gently taxiing along the runway, suddenly sprang into life, the lights dimming as the engines started to roar.

'I hate this bit,' Leah admitted. 'I mean, I know it's the safest form of transport, I know I've got more chance of being killed crossing the road and all that.' She was gabbling now, words spilling out of her mouth as she tried not to think about what was going on. 'I'm fine once it's up, it's just the take-off and landing that sends me into a spin.'

He nodded, turning those lovely eyes to hers, and she waited for a few soothing words to calm her, some tranquil platitude about how he flew all the time, how there was nothing to it, that if the stewards weren't worried then neither was he…

'Take-offs and landings are the most dangerous part.'

She blinked back at him, momentarily taken aback by the callous insensitivity of his statement.

'It's the truth.' Cole shrugged, his eyes idly drifting to the window as Leah shrank back in her seat, screwing her eyes closed as the plane lifted into the late afternoon sky.

'Remind me not to get sick when you're around,' Leah muttered, but he must have had ears on elastic because he turned sharply.

'Excuse me?'

'We'll, you're not exactly sensitive. I bet you're one of those doctors who reel off every last possible complication before you allow a patient to sign a consent form. I bet you list off all the possible side effects before you hand over a script and are only too happy to remind people about the errors of their ways.'

'It's my job.' Cole shrugged again, then gave a rather tight smile. 'Why shouldn't people be informed? Mind you, being an emergency consultant, most of the damage has usually been inflicted long before a patient comes into my care. Still, there's normally a chance for a bit of patient education.'

Suddenly the wedding ring didn't matter a jot. Divine he may be to look at, but his wife was welcome to him, the poor woman!

'We're up.' Those navy eyes were smiling now.

'Oh.'

She'd been so angry she'd forgotten to be frightened, and as the steward wheeled past with the bar Leah thought she'd died and gone to heaven when she was handed a glass with ice and lemon, let alone the hefty gin and tonic that followed a few seconds later. 'Beats Economy.' Leah grinned, taking a sip. 'You have to buzz three times for a glass of water.'

'Cheers.' He lifted up his whisky and soda and after his little lecture, Leah was tempted to play him at his own game, to remind him about the perils of drinking, how that one tiny whisky was killing off brain cells as they spoke, but not sure he'd understand her rather offbeat humour, instead she raised her glass and touched it to his.

'So what do you do?' Cole asked. 'It's only fair you tell me, given I've already told you.'

'I, well, I...' Leah started, toying with whether or not to tell him. The fact he was an emergency consultant and she was an emergency nurse could only lead to one thing—four hours spent discussing work, which was the very thing she was hoping to forget right now. 'A bit of this and a bit of that,' she finished lamely, as Cole looked at her quizzically. 'I've been doing some waitressing, a bit of bar work here and there—enough to save a bit and move on.' She watched a slight frown begin on his forehead and it irritated the hell out of her. Was he such a snob he didn't think she merited a seat next to him? 'I've had a ball in Australia, white-water rafting, bungy-jumping. There wasn't exactly time to hold down a responsible job as well.'

'I've just been to a conference,' Cole responded, and his smile was most definitely derisive. 'You see, I do hold down a responsible job. So responsible, in fact, that we spent the best part of a week discussing your type and the best way to deal with them.'

'My type.' Leah's jaw clanged downwards. Just who did this man think he was? 'And what's my type exactly, Dr Richardson? Are you going to complain to the airline that you were forced to sit next to a lowly waitress and a backpacker to boot?'

'I don't give a damn what sort of work you do,' Cole responded crisply. 'I was talking about tourists that come here and decided to throw all caution to the wind and engage in the types of activity that no normal person would even consider. The type of person that thinks that just because they're on holiday no harm will come to them.'

'And no harm did come to me,' Leah pointed out, taking a grateful sip of her gin as she recalled her one and only bungy-jump and the utter fear that had flooded her as she'd peered over the edge of the raised platform into the tiny river below, remembering how her legs had shaken convulsively as they'd tied the elastic rope around them, how she'd sworn if she only lived to tell the tale she'd never do something so stupid again.

'Obviously.' He gave an on-off smile. 'But if it had, no doubt it would have been *my type* left to pick up and somehow try to put back together the pieces.'

A smart reply was on her lips, a really crushing one, just there for the taking, but even as she thought it, her fury died.

Cole Richardson had a point and, as uninvited as his opinion was, it was a valid one.

It was all very well for her alter ego to sit here and argue the merits of scaling walls and jumping off manmade platforms in an eternal search for adrenaline but the real Leah Jacobs was every bit as jaded with the world as the doom-and-gloom merchant sitting beside her.

Every bit as tired of picking up the pieces of other people's lives.

Leah Jacobs, emergency nurse and Miss Responsible to boot, had burnt out every last piece of emotional reserve after four years in charge of a busy emergency department, had frazzled away every last piece of the cast-iron shield that got emergency nurses through.

This year hadn't just been a long dreamed-of holiday.

This year had been her saviour.

The rather strained silence that followed was thankfully broken by arrival again of the steward. 'Something to make your flight a bit more comfortable.'

Leah fell on the little black bag like a child at Christmas. Pulling open the Cellophane in her haste to get to the goodies within, attempts at sophistication dissolved completely as she moaned in pleasure at the little bottles and jars that fell into her lap. 'Lip balm, moisturiser—oh, and, look, a proper toothbrush, not one of those collapsible ones. Aren't you going to open yours?' she asked as Cole tucked his into the seat pouch.

'I've already brushed my teeth, and as for lip balm…' He gave a vague shrug, then pressed his call bell. Before the light had barely gone on the attentive steward was back. 'Could I have my eye mask, please?'

'Certainly, Doctor, but, we're actually just about to serve dinner.'

Cole shook his head. 'I'll have the eye mask now, please.' And before she even got the words out Cole answered the steward's question. 'I don't want to be woken for meals, thanks.'

And without so much as a goodnight he pushed a button, the chair tilting backwards as he slipped on his mask, not even pulling over himself the fluffy little blanket the steward had returned with, as he effectively dismissed her.

Well, good riddance, Leah thought, casting a ravenous eye over the menu, scarcely able to believe her good luck at being upgraded, though knowing the next leg of her journey home was going to be sheer misery after sampling the delights behind the navy curtain. Still, as annoying as he was, as pompous and opinionated as he had been, she sort of missed Cole as he slept, would have loved to have had someone to sing the praises to about the delicious Australian lamb that was served, the tiny new potatoes and the heavenly chocolate mousse that followed.

Would love to have had someone to sob into her napkin with during the movie as she snuggled into *her* blanket, his gentle snore not even annoying. Stealing a look, she actually felt sorry for him.

Imagine being so blasé, so used to all this, it didn't even merit a glance. What was the point in flying Business Class if you didn't even stay awake for it?

'We're here.'

Opening her eyes, Leah attempted to orientate herself, grumbling at the intrusion, snuggling deeper into her warm blanket. If she could have found a snooze button, she'd have hit it. Still, staring into the dark eyes of Cole wasn't exactly a rude awakening and she smiled sleepily back at him.

'I fell asleep.'

'You certainly did,' Cole agreed.

'Did I snore?' Leah checked, and as per usual he didn't spare her feelings.

'Like a train.'

'Welcome to Melbourne,' the captain broke in, and a long spiel followed about car hire and hotels as Leah blinked a few times, stretching like a cat.

'Did I miss anything?' Cole frowned at her question. 'I mean, did I miss any meals or—?'

'Just coffee and chocolates.' Seeing her face slip, obviously enjoying her torture, Cole elaborated in detail as the plane taxied to its designated landing bay. 'It wasn't much, just a little mini-box, dark, white and milk chocolate, you know the type.'

'No, I don't,' Leah muttered. 'And given this is my one and only foray into Business Class, I doubt I ever will.'

'Here.' Handing her a box, a smile crept over his impassive face as Leah gave a whoop of joy. 'I told the steward I'd give it to you when you woke up. I had a feeling you wouldn't want to miss out.'

The cabin crew were setting up for disembarking now, the seat-belt sign pinging as weary passengers stood up, reaching overhead and pulling out their luggage. As Cole jumped up, Leah suddenly didn't want the journey to end. There was something about him that enthralled her, something behind that rather arrogant exterior she wanted to explore.

'Have a safe trip back to England.' His hand was out again, the gold band flashing its warning light, and Leah purposefully switched off her emotions.

'Thanks.' Shaking his hand, she gave him a smile. 'Sorry about the snoring.'

Have a nice life, she wanted to add as Dr Drop-Dead Gorgeous made his way down the aisle and out of her life, leaving her curiously deflated. Catching sight of his unopened goody bag still sitting in the pouch in front of his seat Leah simply couldn't help herself. The cleaners would only chuck it out, she assured herself as she reached forward and picked it up. It seemed such a shame to waste it.

'Forgot my mobile.'

Jumping as if she'd been scalded, Leah thought she'd die of shame as Cole caught her red-handed. 'Here, I was just picking these up for you. I thought I might see you at customs…'

'It's an internal flight,' Cole pointed out, and she was positive, despite his bland expression, that he was laughing at her. 'Help yourself.'

So she did!

Still burning with embarrassment, she made her way off the plane along the endless corridor and despite her best intentions she found herself scanning the masses for his dark-suited shoulders. He wasn't exactly hard to locate as he stood a good head and shoulders above normal mortals, but catching sight of Kathy's expectant face Leah's attempt at a temporary diversion faded, the sight of her best friend after all this time overriding the pleasure derived from observing a stranger.

Kathy must have seen her as her hand was waving frantically as she dashed forward, her face shining, every bit the bride-to-be, but Leah realised as Kathy threw herself onto Cole that their brief meeting hadn't quite ended.

'Leah,' Kathy shrieked, discarding Cole and lurching forward. 'Can you believe you're here?'

'Not really.' Leah laughed, blushing even more as Cole's questioning eyes turned to her.

'This is Leah,' Kathy introduced them, 'my one and only bridesmaid. This is Cole, the best man, and of course you've already met Dale.'

'The husband-to-be.' Leah kissed him on the cheek as Cole watched her thoughtfully, her own cheeks scorching with pleasure or embarrassment, she truly couldn't decide. 'Are you nervous yet?'

'Not a bit.' Dale grinned. 'So how was the conference, Cole?'

'Long,' Cole said with a dry note to his voice.

'And the flight?'

'Long,' he said again, as Leah burned with indignation.

Kathy, oblivious to the tension, shepherded them out of the arrivals lounge and into the late afternoon sun.

'Isn't he divine?' Kathy nudged Leah as the guys walked on ahead, and Leah knew she wasn't talking about her fiancé!

'Married,' Leah pointed out.

'Widowed.' Kathy winked, reverting to the type of shorthand best friends did so well, and suddenly Leah's pulse kicked into overdrive, but even though men, or lack of them, was usually their favourite topic of conversation there was a certain reluctance on Leah's part to let Kathy know that there was even a hint of attraction.

Kathy's none-too-subtle attempts at matchmaking could only be embarrassing. And, anyway, Leah reminded herself, she was flying back to England on Sunday and as gorgeous as Cole Richardson might be to look at, he wasn't exactly a master of smooth talk.

'Forget it,' Leah said instead. 'I sat next to him on the plane and his company wasn't exactly riveting.'

'Really?'

'Really,' Leah groaned. 'And, believe me, Kathy. Dr Killjoy doesn't do a thing for me. If I want to feel like a naughty schoolgirl then I'll go back to school.'

They were at the car now, but the prospect of a night apart from her beloved Dale had Kathy promptly discarding her manners and she jumped in the front with her fiancé, leaving Cole to lower his six-foot-three frame into the rather cramped back seat as Leah sat rigid, pretending to look out of the window.

'We seem destined to sit next to each other,' he said with a thin smile, which Leah returned with an equal lack of enthusiasm, determined not to let him glimpse that he was having any effect on her whatsoever.

'Did you do any nursing up in Queensland?' Kathy called from the front seat.

'No.'

'Saving yourself for good old London?'

'You said you were a waitress,' Cole pointed out as Kathy giggled at something Dale said.

'I was a waitress in Queensland,' Leah responded through gritted teeth. 'I wasn't aware when you asked what I did for a living that you wanted me to reel off my entire résumé.'

'I didn't.' Cole shrugged, ending the uncomfortable conversation. The rest of the journey was spent rolling their eyes in the back as the happy couple giggled and simpered, and only when they pulled up at a smart town house did Leah and Cole let out long sighs of relief now this embarrassing journey was over.

'Look after him,' Kathy said, turning her head for the first time away from her fiancé. 'No wild parties for his last night of freedom, no shaving off his eyebrows or tying him to the boom gates.'

'I don't think Cole would be so irresponsible,' Leah said with a rather tart edge to her voice. 'You've got nothing to worry about, Kathy.'

Heaven knows why, but the child locks were on in the back and they had to sit through a few uncomfortable minutes as the happy couple said goodbye, and even though they'd be seeing each other the next day, one could have been forgiven for thinking Kathy was waving Dale off to war for all the passion and drama as they bade each other farewell. Mind you, not a lot of talking was going on and Leah and Cole politely stared out of the window for the first half of the performance before finally rolling their eyes at each other.

'Will it never stop?' Leah whispered, and Cole's lips twitched into a smile.

'Get me out of here,' Cole mumbled as the windows steamed up.

'Do you want a chocolate?' Leah giggled, handing him the box he had salvaged for her.

Finally it was over. Dale opened the rear door and Cole and Leah jumped out as Kathy slid over into the driver's seat.

'Enjoy your night in the honeymoon suite.' Dale grinned.

'I feel so guilty.' Leah made a token protest. Kathy and Leah were going to be spending the pre-wedding night glamming themselves up in the honeymoon suite. A two-night deal had been part of the package for booking the reception at the grand hotel, but apart from collecting his cases around eleven p.m. on the night of the wedding Dale wasn't even going to get his toe though the door. Once the happy couple had been safely waved off, Leah had generously been given the run of the honeymoon suite as well as breakfast in bed. The prospect of such a grand ending to her trip after a year sharing dormitories and rooms in youth hostels was a treat indeed. Any attempt at underplaying it soon ended as she started to laugh. 'Actually, I don't feel guilty a bit, just wonderfully spoilt and terribly lucky. Is this your and Kathy's house?'

'I wish,' Dale sighed. 'Ours still only has half a roof. Hopefully a three-month honeymoon in Europe will give the builders time to finish the renovations. Cole offered me his sofa for my last night of freedom.' His eyes strayed back to the car, lingering on Kathy for a second too long. Simultaneously Cole and Leah snapped into action, determined that the good-byes had already been said.

'Isn't he gorgeous?' Kathy said dreamily, staring into the rear-view mirror as the car pulled off. And from the tone of her voice Leah knew that this time the conversation had switched to Dale.

'Hey, if you want to make it up the aisle in one piece tomorrow, I'd suggest you keep your eyes on the road!' Leah said quickly, 'But, yes,' she added, forcing herself not to turn around for one final glimpse. 'He is gorgeous.'

Only she wasn't referring to the groom!

As wonderful as backpacking had been for Leah, as emotionally cleansing and spiritually uplifting as it had been, her time drifting through the red centre and up the east coast of Australia had had its downside.

The mortgage on her tiny yet phenomenally expensive London flat had been taken care of, along with the rates and bills. She'd even paid her little sister to come in and do the occasional dust—preferably after the wild parties she was undoubtedly holding there—but something had had to go and her meticulous budgeting had been to the detriment of her beauty routine.

She wasn't vain or anything, but waxing, manicuring and a six-weekly trim at the hairdresser's didn't really get a look in with the rather frugal budget Leah had set herself.

If ever a major repair job was called for, it was now, but thankfully Kathy had the next twenty-four hours planned down to the last detail in the massive bridal folder she had acquired, which she constantly referred to.

'Bliss,' Leah sighed.

Trimmed, plucked, waxed and massaged to within an inch of their lives, they sat wrapped in huge fluffy white robes, their toenails separated by wads of cotton wool, sipping on champagne as the room-service waiter cleared away the remains of a sumptuous dinner.

'I feel like a muddy old car that's been through a car wash and come out all vacuumed and sparkling. I just hope that I do that gorgeous dress you've chosen for me justice tomorrow!'

'You honestly like it?' Kathy checked for the hundredth time.

'Like it? I love it!' Leah said firmly, and for the first time in bridesmaid history she wasn't lying. Even though she'd mentally prepared herself to smile and coo at the undoubtedly horrendous creation, thankfully on this occasion it hadn't been needed. Leah had long since passed the three-times-a-bridesmaid stage and if she'd learnt anything at all from the experiences it was that no amount of grimacing or subtle suggestions was going to change the outcome. She'd been squeezed into more puffballs than she cared to remember but thankfully at last she was going to walk down the aisle in style. 'Finally a bride with taste!' Leah added, as Kathy waddled like a penguin with her damp toenails to the wardrobe and pulled the simple lilac velvet dress down from the wardrobe door again.

'You're not just saying that so I won't get upset.'

'I promise,' Leah insisted. 'How could I not like it? There's not a sequin or a glimmer of diamanté in sight.'

'And not a single bow,' Kath added proudly. 'Did you manage to find a backless bra?'

'I did,' Leah sighed. 'Though it should come with a user manual. It reminds me of one of those awful sanitary belts from the Dark Ages.'

'At least you need a bra,' Kathy moaned, looking down at her rather flat chest.

'You're going to look divine.' Leah grinned. 'What does your bridal folder say we should be doing now?'

'Sleeping, though I don't fancy our chances. I'm so excited I don't think I'll get a wink all night.'

'Come on.' Pulling back the counterpane, Leah climbed into the massive four-poster. 'We don't want to have bags under our eyes tomorrow.'

'I guess.' Reluctantly Kathy climbed in. 'I wonder what Dale's doing now? You don't think Cole would have taken him on one last wild night out?'

'I doubt it,' Leah muttered. 'I don't think Cole would know what a wild night was if it came up and poked him in the eye.'

'He's really got to you, hasn't he?'

'I just can't stand those know-it-all types who go around spoiling other people's fun.'

'But Cole's nothing like that,' Kathy insisted.

'You didn't sit next to him on the plane,' Leah pointed out. 'You should have heard the lecture he delivered when he found out I'd been bungy-jumping. Talk about kill a conversation dead in two seconds flat.'

'He's just a bit straight-laced,' Kathy relented. 'Mind you, I can't say I blame him.'

'Because he works in Emergency?' Leah argued. 'We work in Emergency and we don't walk around policing everyone, warning them off every tiny risk, every possible side effect.'

'I didn't mean that.' Kathy shook her head. 'Dale says he's changed since his wife died. She was killed in some boating accident or something, that's all I know. Cole never really talks about it. I think it's just been since then.'

Oh, she'd have loved to have probed, would have loved a bit more insight, but Kathy was yawning now, the day catching up with her, her mind drifting towards her wedding day tomorrow, and Leah knew it was neither the time nor the place.

'If I don't get a chance to say it tomorrow, thanks for asking me to be your bridesmaid, for organising the dress and shoes and this wonderful room for me. I feel awful. I'm supposed to be helping you...'

'You'll do the same for me when it's your turn,' Kathy murmured sleepily, and Leah rolled her eyes into the darkness.

'You might have to wait a while for me to return the favour.'

'Are you looking forward to going back? To nursing, I mean.'

There was a long pause, and when Leah finally answered her voice was barely a whisper. 'No.' The sharp sting of tears caught Leah unawares and, aghast, she blinked them back. Tonight was about Kathy, not the absolute mess her life was in right now.

'You'll be all right,' Kathy said gently, her voice sleepy. 'As awful as what happened to you was, it's not going to happen again. Lightning never strikes twice.'

'Oh, yes, it does,' Leah sighed. 'Remember that guy who came into the department...' Her voice trailed off, the soft snores coming from Kathy telling Leah she'd lost her audience. Rolling on her side, she stared into the darkness, not even bothering to wipe the salty tears that slid into her hair.

'Oh, yes, it does,' she whispered softly.

CHAPTER TWO

'THE one thing you asked me to do,' Leah groaned, 'and I managed to mess it up.'

'It doesn't matter.' Kathy giggled, spinning Leah around and shaking her head. 'But you really can't wear that bra. Even with it safety-pinned to your knickers, you can still see the straps.'

You could too. Craning her neck, Leah peered into the full-length mirror. As gorgeous as the strappy dress might be, its plunging back left no room for even the most backless of backless bras.

'The sales assistant assured me no matter how low the dress, this would be OK.'

'She lied.' Kathy giggled again and Leah joined her in a reluctant smile. 'Don't worry.' Pulling at the zipper on one of her suitcases, Kathy pulled out an impressive-looking first-aid box.

'Are you expecting to open a mobile theatre on your travels?' Leah asked.

'There's nothing wrong with being prepared. Anyway, we're heading off the beaten track a bit on our honeymoon. Here it is.' Pulling out a roll of three-inch surgical tape, she registered Leah's look of horror. 'Everyone uses it.'

'Since when?'

'Come on, Leah,' Kathy urged, 'we haven't got time to mess around.'

They hadn't, so rather reluctantly, and blushing to the roots of her smooth blonde hair, Leah suffered the indignity of holding up her rather impressive bosom as Kathy set to work with the surgical tape, jacking up her friend's breasts until an acre of cleavage barely moved an inch.

'It works!' Leah grinned. 'It actually works.'

'You're not allergic to tape, are you?' Kathy checked.

'I don't care if I am,' Leah answered as she slipped back into her dress and pulled up the zipper. 'It looks great.'

They stood for a couple of moments admiring their reflections in the mirror until the phone rang and they were gently reminded that there was a room full of people and an anxious groom waiting downstairs for them.

'You look stunning,' Leah whispered, her eyes filling with tears as she fiddled with Kathy's veil. 'You're the most beautiful bride I've ever seen.'

'And the best bit is that I get to do it all again when we get to England.'

Walking behind Kathy, Leah blushed as she always did when people looked at her. There wasn't a single familiar face in the crowd to give her an encouraging smile unless she counted Cole Richardson, but his smile wasn't exactly encouraging. He gave her a brief glance before turning his attention to the bride and groom, playing the part of the best man to a T as Leah stood beside him, trying to ignore how heavenly he looked in his dark grey suit, trying to remain un-moved by the heady scent of his cologne, which easily overpowered the gorgeous flower arrangements. There was not even one nervous pat of his pocket to check for the rings as he stood supremely confident, dwarfing her with his height as they shared the order of service. Leah's hands trembled as she tried to read the blur of words in front of her.

She always cried at weddings. Even when she wasn't particularly attached to the couple, there was something about the grandeur of the event, watching two people pledging their love, embarking on life's journey together, which made her arms tingle with goose-bumps and tears test her waterproof mascara to its limit.

Unfortunately, as gorgeous as her lilac dress might be, there was absolutely nowhere to hide a tissue and Leah tried to sniff subtly, praying her nose wouldn't start to run. But God must've been concentrating on the ceremony and when dignified sniffs wouldn't suffice, trying to catch Cole's eye remained her only option.

'Have you got a tissue?' she whispered frantically as Cole stared ahead, frowning at the intrusion.

'What?'

'A tissue?' Leah begged, desperately trying not to sniff too loudly.

'Oh, God,' he muttered when finally he turned and faced her, no doubt appalled at the vision that greeted him. 'You'll have to use this.'

Cringing at the prospect of Kathy's wrath, she accepted the gorgeous lilac silk handkerchief that perfectly matched her dress and was supposed to poke out of the top pocket of his suit.

'Try and keep one corner clean,' he hissed out of the side of his mouth.

Leah did her best, but it was a rather sad-looking effort that hung out of Cole's pocket as they lined up for the photographers for the seemingly endless photos. Finally it was over and they sat down to a sumptuous meal before the inevitable speeches, which seemed to go on for ever, finally got under way. Cole's was easily the best, Leah decided, witty without being embarrassing, endearing without being gushing. Best of all, he kept it short and Leah sipped at her coffee liqueur as she watched him, smiling reluctantly at his jokes, her cheeks curiously flushed as she recalled their four hours alone on the plane. He entranced her for all the wrong reasons. Pompous, condescending he most certainly was, but there was something else that she couldn't quite put her finger on. It wasn't just his looks, though undoubtedly they spoke volumes, but something about his strength, his dignity. As his speech neared its end, Leah's eyes, which were still stinging from her embarrassing tears earlier, filled up again as she glimpsed the pain behind the rather severe mask Cole wore so well.

'My late wife, Heather, adored Dale, saw him more as a brother than a friend. Despite her sunny nature, where Dale was concerned, none of the girlfriends he dragged to our dinner table for Heather's opinion were good enough…

'Until Kathy breezed into our lives a couple of years ago, that is.'

He cleared his throat and stared at the notes he was reading from for a second too long before continuing.

'After they left we watched them drive off, and when Heather shook her head I waited, waited for Heather to have picked up some fault I'd missed, some glaring glitch in Kathy's character I'd seemingly ignored. Instead, she let out a long sigh then smiled. "That's the one," she said. "That's the one Dale's going to marry." And, though unfortunately she isn't here to see it, Heather, as always, was right and I know that everyone in this room hopes that you're as happy in your future together as Heather predicted you would be.'

Given that the sole handkerchief was safely back in his pocket, Leah had to make do with a couple of deep breaths and a quick sip of her drink. Looking up, she realised the whole room was looking at her and it took a second or two to realise that Cole was at the end of his speech and performing the duty toast to the bridesmaids.

Or bridesmaid!

Blushing crimson, she forced a smile as Cole held up his glass. 'When Dale asked me to be best man, naturally I was thrilled, but never more so than now. The bridesmaid truly looks beautiful.' A tiny smile softened his face as he worked the room. 'And unlike the rest of the guys here tonight, at least I know that I'm guaranteed a dance.

'To the bridesmaid!'

It was a joke, a light-hearted comment to end his speech on, Leah knew that, *knew that*, but as the speeches ended she sat burning with anticipation. Something in his voice, something in the way his eyes had held hers as he'd spoken told her he had meant it, that this would be more, so much more than a duty dance. As the lights dimmed and Kathy and Dale took to the floor for the first dance, Leah's heart rate shot up as Cole approached. Shooting a look up from the refuge of her fringe, there was an expression she couldn't quite read in his eyes and she knew there and then that the attraction she felt was most definitely mutual. As his hot hand closed on hers she could barely catch her breath as she walked alongside him in unfamiliar, impossibly high heels.

They stood shy and awkward for a moment so fleeting it was barely there, then Cole wrapped his hand around her waist and she slid into his embrace. The music carried them around the room and so tall was he, even in heels her cheek only rested on his chest as his deep low voice drifted to her ears.

'I meant what I said. You really do look beautiful.'

Leah gave a small laugh, pulling her head up slightly so he could hear her. 'It's amazing what a posh frock and a few heated rollers can do. I think yesterday was a more accurate version of me.'

'You looked beautiful then.'

Such was the honesty in his voice, such was its impact, Leah forgot they were supposed to be dancing and stilled for a moment.

Cole's admission was obviously having the same effect on him and while the dance floor revolved around them, while couples entwined and moved to the music, for a second or two everything stopped.

'You didn't make me feel very beautiful,' Leah responded, amazing herself at her boldness. 'In fact, you made me feel incredibly irresponsible and rather unworthy.'

He didn't answer, just stared on as Leah's mouth started to move at a hundred miles an hour, nerves catching up with her as her senses kicked into overdrive. 'If I remember rightly, you fell asleep at the first opportunity. After you'd told me off…'

'That was the safer option.' His eyes were on her, burning into her, and she stared right back. Never had she felt such an attraction, never, not even once in her life had she felt such a connection with another person. And it hadn't just happened on the dance floor.

The instant he had appeared at the check-in desk, he had filled her mind. Her token annoyance at him had been just that.

A token, futile defence she had erected.

Even last night, as she had shared in Kathy's last night of single life, her mind had guiltily wandered to the dashing stranger on the plane, scarcely able to believe her luck at the cards fate had dealt, at the chance to see him again the next day.

She should have left it there. He'd registered his attraction, swelled her ego to unimaginable proportions and made the day extra special. And that was all it could be, Leah reminded herself. Tomorrow she was heading back to England. Tomorrow Australia, Melbourne, this wedding would be just another holiday memory to line up with the rest, to pore over the photos with a wistful smile as her real life resumed.

So why was she taking things further? Leah asked herself.

Why was she tossing her fringe back slightly as she looked up? Running a tongue over her glossed lips as she stared into those gorgeous dark eyes? Lowering her voice as she spoke?

'Safer than what?'

She felt his shoulders stiffen under her hands as he gazed back at her. The bridal waltz had long since ended, their duty dance over, yet neither had made a motion to move. Instead, they swayed away, dancing to their own tune, the throb of the band a distant beat as they moved together.

'Safer than getting involved with someone I barely know, someone who's heading off to the other side of the world tomorrow. Is that a good enough answer?'

'I guess it was to be expected.' She registered his frown and gave a small smile. 'You made it very clear you like to err on the side of caution so, yes, I guess it would be pretty stupid to go and do something crazy.'

'What do you mean by crazy?' He was smiling down at her now. She could feel his breath on her cheek, his arms pulling her in tighter as he awaited her answer to his dangerous question.

She felt as if she were back on the bungy-jump platform again. A golden once-in-a-lifetime opportunity, right there for the taking. It would be crazy, she frantically reasoned, crazy and bad and dangerous to go ahead and jump and, despite her adventures abroad, falling hopelessly in lust had been one she'd been only too willing not to succumb to. She'd enough baggage to lug around without a broken heart to boot, and from the break in his voice when he'd mentioned his wife during the speeches Cole had his fair share of baggage too.

Where was her sense of adventure when she really needed it? Leah wondered with a rueful smile. Why couldn't she just throw caution to the wind and succumb to his charms even if it was for just a night?

But therein lay the problem. Casual sex simply wasn't her style and with the clock ticking by, with her departure drawing more imminent with each and every step, Leah knew that a one-night stand was all it could ever be, so it was with reluctance pouring from every cell that she dragged her eyes up to him as the music ended.

'I'd better go and find Kathy.'

Kathy wasn't exactly much help. As the evening wore on time and again she engineered their meetings, time and again they were left alone at the head table. It should have been awkward but it truly wasn't. Cole was so easy to talk to, he made her laugh, made her feel so dammed sexy when he looked at her, watched her mouth move as she spoke, and it took a mammoth effort to drag herself up to the hotel room to help Kathy out of her dress and into her farewell outfit.

Drunk on love and half a bottle of champagne, Kathy had a glint in her eye and a determination that everyone should be as happy as her as they fiddled with their make-up in the mirror.

'It wouldn't just be a one-night stand,' she insisted. 'Cole Richardson is the consummate gentleman. I can't believe he's actually making a move on you!'

'I'm not that bad,' Leah moaned.

'I didn't mean that. It's just that since Heather died he hasn't so much as even glanced at another woman, hasn't shown the remotest interest. He must just adore you, Leah, and I can't bear the thought of him being rejected. You could kiss him at least, have a drink together…'

'In the honeymoon suite,' Leah pointed out, staring at the massive bed, supposedly prepared for the happy couple. Champagne cooling in a bucket, flowers and chocolates on the table—any hope of resistance would be futile. 'Come on, Kathy, I wouldn't last five minutes alone with him. I've never felt like this and pretending it isn't going to end up in bed if we pursue things is pointless.'

'Then go with it,' Kathy begged. 'Cole isn't going to just get up and walk away.'

'I am, though.'

'Why couldn't something come of it? Look at Dale and I…'

'Kathy, I fly back to England tomorrow, for heaven's sake.'

'So cancel,' Kathy said airily. 'Tell them you've got a raging cough and temperature and they won't let you set foot on the plane.'

'Don't be ridiculous,' Leah admonished. 'I haven't got anywhere to stay, I don't know anyone. Anyway, we probably only feel this way, *because* I'm going tomorrow. There's something quite seductive about knowing you'll never meet again. Can you imagine the poor guy's face if I turn around and say I've decided to stay on?'

'Remember the first night Dale took me out?' Kathy asked, her eyes shining. 'We were sharing a flat and he was the Australian visiting locum about to head back down under? Remember what I said when he knocked at the door?'

Leah nodded, a smile wobbling on her lips. 'If I'm not in bed by eleven I'll be home by twelve.'

'And just look at us now!'

'Come on, Mrs,' Leah said slowly. 'I think your husband's waiting to whisk you away.'

Leah hated goodbyes and even though she knew she'd see Kathy soon, tears pricked at her eyes as the crowd all gathered around them for one final kiss and hug. Leah stood slightly back, smiling shyly as Cole joined her.

'You'll be thinking I'm permanently on the verge of tears,' Leah said by way of greeting. 'It's just weddings that do it to me, especially this one.'

'You're really close, aren't you?'

Leah nodded. 'We shared a flat and a bit more besides. There's been a few too many dramas in my life and Kathy's always been there.'

'She still will be,' Cole said gently as Leah sniffed into the lilac handkerchief he produced for the second time.

'I know. Come on, we'd better wave off the car.'

Unfortunately the entire ballroom had the same idea and as the crowd surged forward, so too did Leah, her high heels not exactly providing the most stable of footing. And though Cole's hand shot out to save her, the stone banister caught the brunt of her rib cage as Leah toppled sideways.

'Are you all right?' he asked, pulling her up as the crowd looked on.

'I'm fine.' Screwing her eyes closed, Leah struggled to catch her breath. 'I'm fine,' she said again. 'I'm just embarrassed.'

'Nobody's looking,' Cole said assuredly, his face concerned as he eyed her carefully. 'They're all too busy waving. That was quite a knock…'

'It's nothing,' Leah gasped, wrapping her arms around her chest then shaking her head as tiny little silver spots danced in front of her eyes. Her chest hurt, it really hurt, and she waited for the pain to go. But it wasn't like a stubbed toe, the agony followed by a dizzy relief. If anything, the pain was getting worse, her breath coming out in short painful bursts.

'I can't breathe,' she whispered, only this time embarrassment had nothing to do with the lowering of her voice. A whisper was all she could manage.

'Let me have a look at you.'

'Not here,' she begged, mortified at such an undignified end to such a wonderful evening. Cole swooped her up into his arms in one quick motion and headed up the stairs and across the foyer, nudging the lift button with his elbow and smiling reassuringly down at her as he did so, even managing a tiny joke as she sagged against him.

'If you wanted to see my room…' he smiled down at her '…you really only had to ask!'

CHAPTER THREE

HE WASN'T joking a few minutes later.

As Cole gently lowered her onto his bed Leah shook her head frantically. Hanging her legs instead over the side, she leant forward, resting her elbows on her knees with her head in her hands in a desperate attempt to fill her lungs with air. The pain in her side was an agony in itself yet it barely registered against the awful feeling of suffocation.

'I can't breathe,' Leah gasped, as Cole knelt on the floor beside her. 'I really can't…'

'It's OK, Leah, don't try and talk.' His voice was calm, his eyes holding hers for a second as he picked up the phone. 'Get an ambulance up to room 204. Tell them there's a doctor present and a female patient with a suspected pneumothorax.' The poor person on the other end couldn't have realised the might they were dealing with as they obviously asked a question. 'Just do it!' Cole roared, making even Leah jump, but, sensing her tension, he turned back to her. 'She wanted to send for the hotel's GP,' he offered by way of explanation. 'Just sit tight for a second, Leah, I'll get my bag.'

Thank heavens he was tidy.

Strange, the things you thought when you were struggling to pull air into your lungs, strange how your mind focused on irrelevances rather than face

41

the dire truth. For Leah it was easier to focus on the fact that had her life depended on finding her bag in the next couple of minutes, she might just as well have laid down and died there and then.

Thankfully her dress was backless so there was nothing to remove, and as Cole listened to her air entry she felt the cool steel of his stethoscope as he pressed it against her back.

'I need to listen to your chest.'

Leah would have loved to have argued, loved to have told him she was fine. And as irrelevant as it was at this moment, the fact that her bust was jacked up with several metres of surgical tape wasn't exactly the image she had been hoping to portray. Dying with shame or lack of oxygen, Leah couldn't decide which, she moved forward. His hands located her zip almost instantly, which was no mean feat considering it was concealed in the seam at the side. Cole was obviously a man who knew his way around a woman's dress, Leah thought, but it was her last stab at humour, her last attempt at self-preservation as the lights seemed to dim, the stars that were flickering in her eyes flashed brighter for a second then dimmed, the counterpane she was gripping so tightly seemed to slip out of her hands as she lurched forward. She struggled to fight it to stay awake, to beg Cole to do something, to tell him that she couldn't die here—not in a stranger's bedroom, not half a world away from home, with her breasts wrapped in tape, not when Kathy was just…

'Leah, you have a pneumothorax.' Cole's voice seemed to be coming at her through a fog. 'That's why you're having so much trouble breathing. A rib must have punctured your lung. Now, I can't wait for the ambulance to get here so I'm going to put a needle in. It's going to hurt,' he warned. She could feel his fingers working their way down her rib cage and the coolness of the alcohol as he swabbed her skin. 'It will only hurt for a second,' he implored, 'and after that you'll feel much more comfortable.'

She would have nodded, told him she understood what he was saying, she'd go through anything just to breathe again, but there was no strength left. A pain so vile, so intense Leah truly thought she would vomit, suddenly ricocheted through her as the needle pierced her chest, broke through into her lung, but just as she thought she would surely die, that surely it was all over, she felt the delicious feeling of air dragging into her lungs, the heady taste of oxygen as it seeped through her body and slowly, slowly her world came back into focus.

'You're all right now.' Cole was strapping the needle into place as he spoke. 'Just stay very still while I secure it. An ambulance is on its way.'

'Thank you.' It seemed such a paltry offering, but it was the only two words she could come up with. Even they were too many for Cole.

'Don't try and talk,' he said crisply. 'Once the ambulance gets here they'll give you some oxygen. You must have fractured a rib when you fell.'

'I feel better now,' Leah said faintly, but Cole begged to differ.

'Well, you don't look it.' Lifting her legs up onto the bed, he grabbed at pillows, making a massive arch

around her, and the bliss as she lay back was inde-
scribable. But the oxygen had obviously reached
Leah's brain now as the indignity of sitting naked
from the waist up hit home.

Cole must have read her mind. 'I'll just cover you
up,' he said, heading for the wardrobe and grabbing
an ugly beige blanket.

'Can you—?'

'Get rid of the tape?' Cole finished for her as a
smile so small it was barely there inched over his lips.
'So that's why there's never any when a doctor asks,
the nurses are too busy swiping it!'

It was the last of his smiles, the last glimpse of the
man she was just starting to know, before the doctor
took over as the paramedics roared into the room,
smothering her in leads as they strapped an oxygen
mask on.

'Let's just get her to Melbourne Central,' Cole said
impatiently as the inevitable questions started. 'I've
only got a Gelco in her, she needs a proper chest tube
and an X-ray.'

Something in his voice told Leah he wasn't about
to be argued with and she was right. In no time at all
she was bumping along on the metal stretcher, screwing her eyes closed in embarrassment as they wheeled
her out through Reception and into the flashing ambulance.

'Thank you,' Leah said again, pulling off the mask
and attempting a brave smile.

'You can thank me later,' Cole replied, climbing
into the ambulance behind her and sitting on the tiny
seat. 'Let's just get you to the hospital.'

He didn't have to come, but Leah was so glad he did, so glad there was, if not a familiar face, at least someone who wasn't a complete stranger sitting beside her as the ambulance sped through the dark streets and the wailing sirens told Leah she wasn't quite out of the woods yet.

Even though it was the other side of the world there was a strange comfort to be had in the familiarity of the emergency room, the efficient triage nurse listening intently to Cole's brief handover as they whisked her straight into Resus. Her dress was removed in a second, along with her shoes, and bundled into a bright yellow bag, the monitors bleeping into life as they were turned on and strapped to her.

'Hi, Cole!' A rather senior-looking doctor had finished listening to her chest and addressed her escort. 'I thought you were supposed to be on a night off.'

'When do I ever get a night off?' Cole responded dryly.

Only then did it dawn on Leah they were actually at his hospital and, worse still, in his very own department.

'Leah, my name's Samuel Donovan, I'm the consultant on tonight. Now, I know you're still having a lot of trouble breathing so I'm going to get the history from Cole for now if that's OK and I'll talk to you when you're a bit more settled.'

Leah nodded her consent, an in-depth discussion the last thing she needed right now.

'I just want to check, though, whether or not you're allergic to anything.'

Shaking her head, Leah gripped the mask tighter.

'Any drugs, sticky tape, any reactions to anaesthetic?'

'She's an emergency nurse, Samuel, I think we can take it as a no!'

'OK.' Samuel relented, but only for a moment. 'Any operations?'

Leah nodded, bringing her hand up to her cheek, her words so husky they were barely audible.

'Fractured cheekbone, about eighteen months ago…'

Samuel nodded. He patted her on the shoulder and turned his attention back to Cole. 'So what's the story?'

'We were at a wedding and she fell against a stone staircase. Initially I thought she was winded but she deteriorated pretty rapidly. I've just put in a temporary needle, she'll need a proper chest tube.' He caught her frantic eyes above the oxygen mask. 'And some decent pain control.'

'Sure.'

Whatever they gave her, it worked pretty fast. Finally each breath wasn't such a supreme effort. She was vaguely aware of the chatter going on around her, the cold of the X-ray film behind her back as a portable chest X-ray was quickly taken, the slight sting of the local anaesthetic as they set about inserting a chest drain. Even though Leah braced herself for a repeat of the previous agony she had endured, the chest tube entering wasn't nearly as bad as she had anticipated.

'It's done now,' Cole said gently, when the tube

was finally stitched in place. 'Try and get some rest now.'

'I'd like a quick word first, if I may,' Samuel broke in, but Cole shook his head impatiently.

'She's exhausted. Surely she can rest for half an hour.'

'I really do need to talk to her.'

'I'll be fine.' Leah looked up. 'I feel much better now.'

Cole gave a small shrug, looking over expectantly at Samuel, waiting for him to start taking the history, but when Samuel asked him to wait outside even Leah found herself frowning.

'We shan't be long, Cole,' Samuel said firmly. 'I'd just like to talk to Leah alone.'

'Sure.'

Even the nurse who was hovering by the monitors was asked to wait outside, and when they were finally alone Leah turned her bemused face to the doctor.

'What's wrong?'

'Nothing.' Samuel cleared his throat. 'I just thought it might be easier for you to talk without an audience. Now, do you want to tell me what happened tonight?'

'Like Cole said, we were at a wedding, waving off the bride and groom. Everybody moved forward and I toppled against the staircase.'

'The paramedics said that they were called to a hotel room.'

Only then did the sudden need for privacy dawn on Leah and she shook her head frantically, appalled that Samuel thought Cole could have done this to her.

'No, oh, no, I fell, I really did. I asked Cole to get

me away from everyone. I couldn't bear people watching, especially at a wedding.'

There was the longest silence, Samuel chewing his bottom lip as he stared at her chart.

'Leah, I know this is difficult. It's hard for me too. Cole is my colleague and a friend after all. But you're my patient and it's my job to ask these questions. If there is anything you need to tell me, now would be a good time.'

Again she shook her head.

Again Samuel didn't look convinced.

'There are several old rib fractures on your chest X-ray. They look fairly recent, say eighteen months or so old—around the time you fractured your cheek-bone?' He pushed gently. 'Were you in a car accident?'

Leah shook her head but tears were starting to fall now.

'Were you beaten?'

A tiny nod was all the answer she could manage for a moment or two, but, realising the awful situation she had put Cole in, she struggled against her emotions and 50 milligrams of pethidine to clear his name.

'I only met Cole yesterday. None of this has anything to do with him. He was just doing what any doctor would have done tonight when I fell—he saved my life. The old fractures happened in England...' She was starting to get distressed, the alarms going off as she started to cry.

'It's OK, Leah, I believe you,' Samuel said gently. 'But you do understand why I had to ask. I'll arrange for a social worker to come and talk to you on the ward.'

She struggled to argue, to tell him she didn't need a social worker poking her nose in, that she was fine, just fine, but she simply didn't have the strength. 'Just take a couple of nice slow deep breaths,' Samuel said gently. 'That's the way.'

The nurse was back, concern on her face as she came over and checked the monitors, followed by a rather uptight-looking Cole. 'What the hell did you say to her?' he demanded. 'Look at the state she's in...' His voice trailed off as he eyed the X-ray on the overhead monitor, the old fractures and Samuel's red cheeks pretty much speaking for themselves.

'I'm sorry, Cole,' Samuel said finally when the silence had gone on for way too long. 'You know as well as I do that I had to ask.'

'Oh, Cole,' Leah moaned, when they were finally alone. 'I am so—'

'Don't,' Cole said in a clipped voice. 'I've had Samuel grovelling for the past half-hour. I really don't need a repeat.'

'But even so,' Leah said. 'I've put you in an awful situation.'

'I've been in far worse.' Cole shrugged. 'And even though I haven't told him yet, Samuel was completely right to ask you. Too many times women come through the doors of an emergency room and because their husband's a doctor or a policeman or whatever, no one wants to get involved and do the tough asks. I'm sure you've seen it for yourself.'

Leah gave a glum nod.

'Samuel did well,' Cole carried on. 'He put the patient first, which is exactly what we insist upon here, and I'll tell him the same tomorrow.' His voice softened, his eyes concentrating on Leah's reaction as he spoke. 'Do you want to talk about it—the old fractures I mean?'

She didn't.

'It might help,' Cole suggested, when Leah shook her head. Tears were filling her eyes now, the realization of her situation only really starting to dawn.

'I'm supposed to be flying…'

'I'll ring the airline as soon as I get home.' Cole said quickly. 'If you give me your parents' number, I can ring them too. It's daytime in England so at least they'll be spared a call in the middle of the night.'

'But with this type of injury…' Her mind was working ten to the dozen, the appalling facts speaking for themselves as she did the sums in her head, begging for a respite, praying that she'd got things wrong. But when Cole took her hand and looked her in the eye, when he put on his doctor's voice as he addressed her, Leah knew there and then she was doomed.

'You can't fly, Leah,' Cole said firmly.

'For how long?' she begged.

'It's hard to say,' Cole said evasively, but Leah wasn't having any of it.

'Oh, come on, Cole, cut the doctor talk. I need to know.'

'OK.' His eyes met hers and Leah felt her heart

plummet as he carried on talking. 'Six weeks at best.' He gave a tiny shrug. 'But I think three to six months would be more realistic. Leah, this is a serious injury…'

He must still be talking, Leah registered. She could see his lips moving, hear the occasional reference to cabin pressure, the risk of her lung collapsing in mid-flight, but it was all too much to take in.

Her luggage had been sent on, Kathy would be out of the country by now, all the friends she had made were in Brisbane, her bank account was practically empty…

She was stuck, stuck in this foreign country with no money, no friends and nowhere to stay, with a kaput lung to boot.

Panic welled up in her as Cole begged her to stay calm, to take slow deep breaths. 'It will all be OK,' he insisted, his words assured, his tone matter-of-fact. 'Everything's going to be fine.'

'How can you say that?' Leah sobbed. Never had she felt more alone, more scared, more vulnerable, and there wasn't a single thing she could do, not even the tiniest piece of driftwood to cling to as everything familiar was swept away. Her mind searched for answers, for some shred of comfort, but there was none to be had and Leah turned her panicked eyes to Cole. 'I don't know what to do.'

'There's nothing you can do,' Cole said gently, easing her back onto the pillow. Picking up a hand towel, he ran it under the tap before gently wiping her tear-stained cheeks. 'Except to lie back and concentrate on getting better. Things will all seem better in the morning.'

'Oh, no, they won't,' Leah muttered, but his soothing words were actually helping. She could feel her heart rate slowing, her breathing coming more easily now.

'Yes, they will, Leah,' Cole said. 'The main thing is that you're going to be OK. The other stuff is mere details, and nothing that we can't sort out.'

We.

Closing her eyes, Leah was vaguely aware of him pulling a blanket up around her shoulders, his deep, low voice relaxing her. And even though he surely couldn't mean it, that the *we* he referred to would surely change in the morning, that the pile of problems that had landed in her lap would be hers alone to sort out, it was nice just to give in for a while, to put her problems on hold, to accept his words of comfort and let sleep finally wash over her.

Maybe Cole was right, she mused as his voice faded into the background, as the constant bleeps droned on in the distance.

Maybe things really would seem better in the morning…

Not better exactly, but after talking to her parents and sister things certainly seemed brighter.

'I'm actually glad that you're not coming home,' Kara said with a giggle. 'I don't mean it like that,' she added quickly. 'Of course it's awful that you're sick and everything, but guess what?'

Leah wasn't exactly in the mood for guessing games but she went along with it anyway. 'What?'

'Paul and I are going to move in together. He hasn't been living here, though, well, perhaps the odd night here and there,' she rattled on. 'But we've been looking for a flat for ages and there's nothing, *nothing* we can afford, so if it's OK with you, we'll stay at yours till you come home.'

'That's fine,' Leah sighed. It wasn't as if she had much choice.

'We'll pay rent, of course,' Kara added, and Leah nearly dropped the phone in surprise. Kara never paid for anything, she was constantly trying to borrow a fiver, and hearing her actually volunteer to pay rent was more of a shock to the system than having a chest tube inserted. 'It will be like a trial run.' Kara's excited voice chattered on. 'It will do us good to see if we can really afford to take on a mortgage, so don't worry about a thing.'

'She's right,' Mrs Jacobs said, grabbing the phone and taking it from her younger daughter. 'You just concentrate on getting better. Dr Richardson explained everything very nicely and he also said the last thing you needed right now was to get worked up over small details. Now, your dad and I will wire you some money over. Have you thought of anywhere you can stay?'

'One of the youth hostels has single rooms,' Leah answered. 'I was going to ring them after I'd spoken to you. It's not exactly luxurious but it's a bed and it's clean and they've even got a small canteen so I won't have to worry about cooking.'

'Well, there you are, then, darling,' Mrs Jacobs soothed. 'Everything's taken care of.'

'Not quite.' Leah's voice faltered. 'Could you ring work for me, explain to them what's happened? They're not going to be very thrilled.'

'That's already been done. Dr Richardson took the number and rang them after he spoke to us, he's going to fax through a medical certificate. So enough stressing, Leah, we'll speak to you soon.'

Replacing the receiver, Leah smiled as a very young, very nervous grad nurse, who'd introduced herself as Tara, started to take her blood pressure, probably intimidated by the fact that Leah was also a nurse.

'All normal.' Tara smiled, blushing as she did so. 'What did the doctors say on their ward round?'

'Not much,' Leah sighed. 'Apparently the big boss, Dr Crean, will be back tomorrow for his ward round, but the charge nurse seems to think that the chest tube will hopefully come out tomorrow, and if all goes well I could be home by the middle of the week.' Even as she said it Leah let out a slightly wry laugh. The youth hostel could hardly be described as home, but that was exactly what it was going to be for the next few weeks.

'Looks like you've got a visitor.' Making herself scarce, the grad nurse bade the top of Cole's head good morning and dashed off.

'It's the effect I have on women.' Cole grinned.

'The poor thing's nervous. It's bad enough looking after a nurse without having a consultant watch you write up your obs.'

'I brought you this.' Holding up her rather sad-looking backpack, Cole placed it beside the bed. Have you spoken to your parents yet?'

'Just.' Leah nodded. 'I thought Mum would be having a major panic attack but she actually took it really well—too well perhaps,' Leah added glumly. 'If anything, they all sound quite delighted that I'm not coming home.'

'They're no such thing, so stop feeling sorry for yourself,' Cole scolded lightly. 'Your mum did have that major panic attack you were describing when I called her last night, but I told her she needed to calm down before she spoke to you, that the last thing you needed was more stress, so if she sounded too laid-back for your liking then you can blame me. How are you feeling?'

'Better,' Leah admitted. 'Stupid, but better. I've had a sponge bath, but if my obs are still good later this morning they're going to let me have a shower, so I'm crossing my fingers.'

'Is there anything I can get you, anything you want me to bring in?'

Leah shook her head.

'There must be something.'

'A couple of new nighties.' She grinned. 'But given that I don't possess such a thing, it would be a tough ask. And, no, I don't expect you to drag around the lingerie department, I'll just have to settle for hospital gowns.'

'Lemon suits you.' He smiled, but the smile soon faded and he stood there awkwardly. She could almost feel him wishing his bleeper would go off or her phone would ring. Hospital visits were always pretty strained, and none more so than when you barely knew each other, and now the small talk had clearly run out.

'I just popped up to make sure you were improving.'

'I am.'

'And there's nothing you need...'

'Nothing,' Leah said brightly, too brightly. 'Nothing at all. By the way, thanks for last night, Cole, you saved my life.'

'Just doing my job.'

She could almost feel the sigh of relief when a young woman approached, peering at the name above the bedhead.

'Ms Jacobs?'

'Leah.'

'I'm Jasmine Paine, the social worker. Dr Donovan thought it might be helpful if we have a little chat. I'll just get your notes and I'll be back in a couple of minutes. Perhaps your, er, visitor might like to say goodbye.'

Looking up, Leah couldn't decide who was more embarrassed, the social worker or Cole, but from the blush spreading across his face it was a pretty close call.

'Why the hell do I feel so guilty?' Cole said, for once looking anything but confident. 'She thinks I did this to you, you know.'

'Well, not for much longer. Thanks again, Cole.'

'I'll come and see you later,' he offered, but Leah shook her head.

'There's no need, you really don't have to.' His pager did go off and Leah accepted his apologetic smile with one of her own before he dashed off down the ward.

The social worker seemed curiously disappointed when she found out Leah's injury really was just the result of an accident.

'What about the previous fractures?' she asked with a note of suspicion, obviously not entirely convinced. 'You said on admission that you were beaten.'

'Which I was,' Leah sighed. She really didn't want to go there, really didn't want to open up in the middle of a mixed ward with only a flimsy curtain separating her from her roommates, but she wasn't exactly being given much choice. Perhaps more pointedly she wanted any last smidgen of suspicion to be cleared from Cole, the poor guy certainly didn't deserve it. 'It was a patient that beat me up.' She watched the social worker's reaction, concentrating on keeping her voice even, determined not to give a hint that that fateful night was still affecting her. 'I'm a nurse. I was on duty in Emergency one night and one of the patients suddenly became violent.'

'He fractured your ribs!' The horror in Jasmine's voice was genuine but Leah chose to ignore it. 'And your cheekbone?' she added glancing down at her notes. 'That must have been awful for you.'

'It was,' Leah admitted. 'But not only for me. One of the doctors I was on duty with had his hand stamped on. He was hoping to be a surgeon, but with the damage inflicted that seems a pretty far-off dream now.'

'The hospital pressed charges, I hope?'

Leah gave a small nod. 'They did, but unfortunately it didn't get us anywhere. The patient blamed his head injury, said that he didn't know what he was doing at the time, and he got let off with a good behaviour bond. I left for Australia two weeks after the court case. I just couldn't face working in Emergency any more. Everything just set me on edge—every drunk, every raised voice just made me go cold.'

'Have you seen someone,' Jasmine probed gently, 'spoken to a counsellor?'

Leah nodded. 'My hospital was great. They arranged someone straight away and I suppose it did help a bit, made me put things into perspective…' She chewed on her lip as Jasmine sat there quietly waiting for her to continue. 'Everyone's been great really— the police, the solicitors. Even Admin came to the party and provided extra security guards at night. They've all done their bit.'

'But it isn't quite enough,' Jasmine suggested, but Leah just shrugged.

'I can't walk around with a bodyguard! I know the chances of it happening again are tiny, I know it was just a one-off, I know all that.' Struggling to hold it together, it was a while before Leah continued. 'I just want to forget about it.

'Look, Jasmine, I know you're only trying to help, I know this is your job and that you mean well, but going over and over it doesn't change how I feel. If anything, it makes things worse.'

'Fair enough.' Standing, Jasmine gave her a sympathetic smile, which Leah neither wanted nor needed. 'Here's my card. If you need to talk to someone, or even if you need help arranging accommodation, you can call me.'

'Thank you.' Taking the card, Leah stared at it politely before placing it on her bedside locker as Jasmine turned to go. 'Could you leave the curtains closed, please?' Leah asked as Jasmine started to pull them open. 'I'd like a moment on my own.'

Unfortunately privacy wasn't a priority in hospital and just as Leah let down her guard, just as a good cry about all that had happened seemed imminent, the curtains were whisked open by Tara. 'Time for that shower, Leah. I've got some towels and face washers for you, but do you have a toiletry bag and a nightdress?'

'In my backpack,' Leah answered, hastily wiping her cheeks with the backs of her hands. 'Or at least there's a toiletry bag. I'm afraid I'm going to be wearing gowns while I'm here.'

'But why?' Tara asked. 'What's wrong with these?' Pulling out two brand-new, very cute pairs of cotton short pyjamas, Tara gave her a curious look. 'And this dressing-gown is divine. Why on earth wouldn't you want to wear them?'

'Don't tell me there are slippers in there as well?'

Smiling, Tara held up a pair. 'Did a fairy come in the night?'

'Something like that,' Leah gulped. She had been

joking when she'd said she'd wanted him to go shopping. Never in a million years had it entered her head that Cole might have already done it, and no mean feat on a Sunday morning. He must have gone to one of the major shopping centres.

Levering herself gently off the bed, watching as Tara picked up the chest drain and then the ever-present clamps, which were essential in case the drain tube inadvertently became disconnected, she held onto her drip pole as Tara wheeled her the short distance to the shower, barely able to keep the smile off her face.

Suddenly she didn't feel quiet so alone any more. What had been a wretched morning didn't seem quite so bad all of a sudden.

And it was all down to Cole.

CHAPTER FOUR

'Now you're sure you've got everything?' Tara checked as Leah gingerly levered herself off the bed and into the wheelchair Tara was holding. 'Painkillers, an outpatient appointment for two weeks' time and your doctor's letter?'

'It's all in my bag. Thanks so much for all your help with everything, Tara, you really have been great.'

'You've been a perfect patient.' Tara smiled. 'When I was first allocated to you, I admit that I was terrified. Chest tubes scare me at the best of times…'

'And when they're attached to a nurse, it doesn't exactly help!' Leah smiled. 'How long did the taxi say they'd be?'

'Fifteen minutes or so. Would you like me to wheel you down to the taxi rank now?'

'I'll do it.' Both women looked up as Cole approached, a tired smile on his face but still cutting quite a dash in his inevitable suit.

'There's really no need, Doctor.' Tara flushed. 'I'm more than—'

'It's no big deal,' Cole broke in. 'I was just coming past to say goodbye. The taxi rank is outside Emergency anyway.'

Never had Leah felt more useless. Cole pushed the wheelchair at breakneck speed towards the lift and once inside he stood next to Leah, both staring at the lights flashing past the numbers in strained silence.

It was Cole who broke it first. 'Why are you sulking?'

'I'm not,' Leah replied, forcing a smile and hugging her backpack just a bit tighter.

'I know a sulk when I see one, and you, Miss Jacobs, are definitely sulking.' The lift door pinged and opened, but it didn't faze Cole. He carried on talking as he glided the wheelchair along the highly polished corridor and the only saving grace on offer was the fact he couldn't see her face as he hit the nail right on the head. 'Is it because I didn't come and visit you?'

'Of course not,' Leah lied.

'Because,' Cole carried on, ignoring her response, 'if I remember rightly, you explicitly said that you didn't want me to.'

'I said that you didn't have to,' Leah corrected, blushing ever deeper as she did so.

'And that's why you're sulking?'

Leah shrugged and instantly regretted it, given that it wasn't the most painless manoeuvre with a fractured rib. 'Well how would you like it—stuck for four days in a mixed ward with not a single visitor? All my roommates must have thought that I was some sort of social outcast. It was embarrassing.'

'Then you should have rung down to Emergency— I gave you the extension code. Leah, I'm not a mindreader. You said you didn't want me to visit and I complied, so the next time you need something just ask, OK?'

'OK,' she mumbled, blinking at her first glimpse of the outside world in a while. A horrible bubble of panic welled inside her at the prospect of leaving the boring but safe confines of the hospital ward and dealing with the outside world with a rib cage that felt like a rugby league player's after a grand final game, and not a soul in the world to lean on. Four yellow cabs were lined up at the taxi rank and Leah knew there would be no prolonged goodbyes, probably not even the chance of being asked for a coffee and a catch-up, but, then, why would he? Leah reasoned. She'd been nothing but trouble for Cole since they'd met. The poor guy had practically been accused of domestic violence, thanks to her, there wasn't a reason in the world why he shouldn't just bundle her into a taxi and give her a cheery wave goodbye as he rolled his eyes in relief.

'The taxi rank is back there.' Leah gestured, turning frantically as they whizzed past it.

'I'm well aware of that.' He didn't elaborate, just carried on pushing her until they arrived at what was clearly the doctor's car park, given the massive RESERVED signs. As they pulled up at a rather impressive dark blue sports car which, given he was opening the boot and flinging her backpack in, Leah assumed must be Cole's!

'You don't have to drive me to the youth hostel,' Leah groaned. 'A taxi would be fine.'

'I have no intention of driving you to the youth hostel,' Cole responded in a matter-of-fact voice. 'You're coming to stay at my house.'

'Don't be ridiculous,' Leah started, but Cole was having none of it.

'No, Leah,' he said sharply. 'Ridiculous is trying to recuperate after a serious chest injury in a youth hostel of all places. Ridiculous is trying to get some rest with a hundred backpackers determined to party into the small hours every night and ridiculous is thinking you'll get through the next few weeks without picking up every cough, cold and bug that's floating around the place.'

'It's very clean.'

'I know that,' Cole responded. 'I went and checked it out for myself, but it's the last place a woman in your condition should be. Surely you can see that?'

Wearily Leah rubbed her forehead. She *could* see that, she wasn't stupid after all and the prospect of lying on a hard bed in a single room for the next few weeks as parties raved on outside didn't hold much charm. There was only a communal television room and, Cole was right, at any given time someone had a roaring cough or cold—not the ideal place to get well in. 'It just seems such an imposition,' Leah said lamely. 'You barely know me.'

'You'd do the same, though?' Cole ventured. 'If the same thing had happened to a friend of Kathy's and Dale's in England?'

'Of course,' Leah answered without thinking, 'but it's not the same, is it?' She looked at his uncomprehending face, cringing with mortification as she continued but knowing the air had to be cleared. 'Cole, we got on really well on the night of the wedding.'

'Which will make living together easier,' he said.

He wasn't making this easy. 'I'm worried you might think…'

'Think what?'

'Well…' Leah gave a small cough. 'I was supposed to be heading back to England the next day. It was a lot easier to get on then, you know, no commitments, no strings…'

'You think I'm doing this so I can sleep with you?'

'Of course not.' Leah flushed. 'I'm just pointing out that back at the wedding, well, it would have been for one night and suddenly you're stuck with me for the next few weeks.'

'From one-night stand to live-in girlfriend?' Cole asked, a tiny grin on his lips.

'Something like that,' Leah mumbled.

'You turned me down,' Cole pointed out. 'You made it very clear that romance wasn't on your agenda.'

She wanted to correct him, to tell him that romance was very much on her agenda, it had been a one-night stand she had been opposed to, but instead she stayed quiet. She had some pride left after all, albeit not much!

'I just can't come and stay with you,' Leah said, though not as firmly as she would have liked, admitting to herself that if he pushed again she'd give in gracefully and accept. Looking up, she was slightly startled as he unloaded the backpack and handed it to her before pushing the wheelchair in the direction of the taxi rank.

'Up to you,' he said abruptly. 'The last thing I want is a kidnapping charge on top of the alleged assault.'

The taxis were looming ever closer, there wasn't even a queue to delay her departure, and Leah had to think fast. 'Oh, OK, then,' she wailed, trying to sound as if she was relenting. 'If it makes you feel better.' But she wasn't getting away with it that easily.

'Don't worry about how I feel.' Even though she couldn't see him, she knew that he was laughing at her. 'It has to be your choice. Now, Leah, I'll ask you once again—would you like to come and stay with me?'

'Yes,' Leah mumbled, though not very graciously. 'Yes, please.'

It felt strange to be back at Cole's smart town house. Even though it had been only a few short days since she'd seen it, so much seemed to have happened since then.

Accepting his hand, she slowly got out of the car. Walking wasn't so much of a problem, it was standing up or sitting down that seemed to require a mammoth effort. Still, even the few steps from the car to the front door had Leah slightly breathless and it had nothing to do with Cole!

'There's a downstairs bathroom,' Cole pointed out as they stepped inside, 'but I'm afraid the two bedrooms are both upstairs. I could make up a bed on the sofa, though it's a bit small,' he added doubtfully, but Leah quickly shook her head.

'Upstairs will be fine. I'll just take my time getting there, that's all. Dr Crean said that gentle exercise was good.'

He was the perfect host, showing her every downstairs room, the temperamental gas stove, even where spare loo paper was kept, doing everything he could to make her feel welcome. 'There's a lap pool outside,' Cole gestured and Leah's face lit up, visions of going back to England with a tan *and* toned thighs brightening the day dramatically. 'Not that you'll be using it. Rest and more rest is the order of the day.'

'For now, but in a couple of weeks…'

'No swimming,' Cole ordered, and Leah gave a small moan of protest, though her heart wasn't in it. She could barely keep the smile off her face. Cole's home was certainly more inviting than the youth hostel and as she wandered around Leah found herself wondering who had come up with the colour scheme. It was a brave person indeed who had painted the walls jade, but it actually worked. 'Here's the study.' Stepping inside, Leah gazed at the book-lined walls. Books brought a certain comfort, a feeling of homeliness, and she wandered over to the shelves, staring for a moment or two at the endless rows that lined the shelves. 'Help yourself if anything catches your eye.'

'Everything catches my eye,' Leah admitted. 'You'll be stuck with me for the next decade, I'm afraid. There's loads of books here I can't wait to read.'

'Just as well.' Cole smiled. 'There's not much else you can do. Still, there's the computer so you can have a surf, fire off a few emails and tell everyone what's happened. There's not much food in, I'm afraid, I didn't get time to do a shop.' He gave a low laugh. 'Actually, I never shop, I live on take-aways, but I'll hit the supermarket at the weekend. Still, I got some bread, milk and cheese from the milk bar and we can ring out for something when I get home.'

'You're going back to work?'

Cole nodded. 'I just slipped out for an hour; I thought it might be easier for you to settle in without me here.'

'Look, about rent,' Leah started. 'I can't afford much, but—'

'Leah.' Cole shook his head. 'Please, don't embarrass me. You don't have to pay to stay here.'

'Well, at least let me give you what I would have paid at the youth hostel.'

But Cole wouldn't hear of it. 'I don't want any money. And while we're on embarrassing subjects, please, Leah, I don't want you to feel uncomfortable, I want you to treat the place as home. I'm barely here so it's not as if we're going to see much of each other.'

She almost said 'Pity' but, given the 'just friends' lecture he had delivered in the car park, thought better of it.

'I'll be back around nine. Now, you'll be OK?'

'I'll be fine.'

'The hospital number and my pager number are by the phone.' He glanced at his watch. 'I really do have to go.'

'Then go.' Leah smiled. 'And, Cole, thanks for this, I really mean it.'

As he turned to go she called him back. 'I'll need your password.'

'Password?'

'For the computer. I was going to email Mum.'

'Oh.' He cleared his throat and Leah could have sworn he nearly blushed. 'It's "tiger."'

'Thanks.'

'I'll see you, then,' Cole said, beating a hasty retreat as Leah hobbled down the corridor, just making it to the front door as he stepped into his car.

'See you tonight.' Leah grinned. 'Tiger!'

CHAPTER FIVE

'WHAT'S the smell?' Sniffing the air, Cole put down his briefcase, a curious smile on his face.

'Dinner,' Leah answered. 'What are you smiling at?'

'It just seems strange.' He gave a small shrug. 'Coming home with the lights on and the television blaring.'

'Nice strange?' Leah checked, and Cole gave a small nod.

'Nice strange,' he admitted, but then his voice changed, the authoritarian note creeping back. 'How on earth did you make dinner? There isn't a single tin of anything in the cupboards. You weren't stupid enough to go shopping, I hope?'

'Only on the internet. And before you tell me off, the delivery man brought all the boxes through to the kitchen, I only had to put things away.'

'But you're supposed to be resting,' Cole protested—and quite strongly too, opening the cupboards and shaking his head. 'I didn't bring you here to have you act like an unpaid housekeeper. I don't expect you to buy my groceries, for heaven's sake.'

'They're *my* groceries,' Leah answered tartly, not remotely fazed by his annoyance. 'But because you're being so nice to me, I'll let you share. I'd have had to do the same thing at the youth hostel,' she carried on, refusing to let him get a word in. 'Well, actually, I'd have had to *go* shopping, because there isn't a computer for the inmates, then I'd have had to lug the whole lot home and write my name on everything before placing it in the fridge, and then no doubt some hairy creature would have got up in the middle of the night with the munchies and eaten the lot and I'd have been back where I started. So, you see, it's really no trouble, no trouble at all. In fact, it's a pleasure.'

'So what is it?' Cole asked, only slightly mollified.

'What's what?'

'For dinner?'

Opening the cooker, Leah peered inside. 'Leah's chicken surprise with jacket potatoes.' Turning, she gave a smile at his bemused expression. 'But you'll have to lift the casserole dish out for me.'

They ate on the sofa, their plates precariously balanced on their knees, watching the latest reality TV show, which had Leah enthralled and Cole bored to tears.

'They know the cameras are there,' he pointed out. 'As if they're going to do something stupid when the whole wide world can see.'

'But the cameras are hidden,' Leah answered, her eyes avidly pinned to the screen. 'After a couple of days they forget all about them. I tell you, boyfriend or not, those two are going to end up sleeping together. I'm an expert on relationships.' She gave a low laugh. 'At least I am on other people's. When it comes to me I always get it wrong.'

'So I take it from that there's no one waiting for you back home?' She was aware of his head turning towards her and suddenly the screen seemed to blur into the background, the intensity of his gaze scorching her cheek, and she knew, just knew, that as casual as his question had sounded, the answer really mattered.

'My family, of course.' Turning, she gave him a mischievous smile, daring him with her eyes to push further.

'And?'

'And my friends, of which there are quite a few.'

'I'm sure there are.' She watched his Adam's apple bob in his throat and resisted the urge to put him out of his misery, determined for once in her life to play it cool, to be absolutely certain Cole wasn't merely making small talk. 'Anyone else?'

'Well, there's Ben,' Leah said lightly. 'Apparently he's missed me a lot.'

'Ben?'

Leah nodded. 'But he's very forgiving. I'm sure things will be fine when I get home.'

'Have you been together long?'

'Four years.' Leah chewed on her lip. 'Actually, it's coming up for five soon.'

'Do you live together?'

'Heavens, no.' Leah shook her head. 'My flat's not big enough.'

'But it's serious between the two of you?' Cole checked, and something in his eyes told Leah she wasn't the only one losing her cool here, that the signs were so blazingly clear a blind man couldn't have misinterpreted them.

'Of course it's serious.' A tiny smirk curled the

corner of her mouth. 'One should never get a pet without giving it a lot of thought, everyone knows that. Ben's mine but he stays at my parents' house, they've got a decent-sized back garden.'

'Ben's a dog?'

Leah nodded, watching as he darted his eyes back to the screen and changed the subject with a small embarrassed cough.

'We won't have to watch it, I hope? When those two finally get it on, I mean,' Cole said gruffly, taking a slug of Coke.

'Of course we'll watch it, but don't worry.' Leah grinned. 'If it happens while you're at work, I'll tape it for you.'

'I can hardly wait.'

Cole cleared the dishes, shooing Leah away when she tried to help. 'It's your first night out of hospital, for goodness' sake, sit down and relax. Surely you're tired?'

'Not really,' Leah admitted. 'I've done nothing but sleep for four days. I even had a doze on the sofa this afternoon.'

'Good!' Cole said. 'You need to rest. I've made up the bed in the spare room—I hope it's comfortable enough.'

'Anything will be comfortable after sleeping on a rubber mattress in the hospital with the whole ward snoring, and I can guarantee it will be better than the youth hostel.'

Loading the dishwasher, he stopped midway and looked at her for a moment or two before speaking.

'Would you be offended if I say that you don't look much like a backpacker?'

'Mortally,' Leah said, grinning. 'Actually, I never felt like a backpacker. I like my home comforts too much. I kept wanting to put photos up in the dormitories and things. The people at the hostel sort of fell into three groups, those out for a wild party—'

'Don't you like parties?' Cole asked.

'On the contrary, I love a good party, it's just my version tends to differ from theirs. I like standing around in a strappy dress sipping wine and talking, whereas...' She levered herself up from the sofa and performed an impromptu wild sort of motion, flinging her arms in the air and rolling her eyes back in her head, and even though it hurt like hell, the pain was worth it for the smile it raised from Cole. 'I think my clubbing days are long since over.'

'What were the others like?' Cole asked, forgetting to put the dishwashing tablet in as he closed the door and programmed the machine.

'Oh, the hearty type. Up at the crack of dawn and setting off in serious walking boots, poring over maps at the dinner table, in bed by eight, you know the sort. I didn't fit in with them either. Apart from my runner's shorts and bathers, my backpack contained a cocktail dress and stilettos...' She was gabbling now. Cole had finished with the dishwasher and was walking towards her, and suddenly there was no dinner to serve up, no table to lay, no dishes to be done, not a single diversion to be had. And Leah really needed one. There was something in his eyes she couldn't read, a certain hesitancy in his movements, and Leah frantically dragged her mind away from how divine he looked, how effortlessly sexy he really was, and rattled on, the slightly breathy note to her voice for once having nothing to do with her bruised rib cage. 'Not that I got to wear them—the stilettos, I mean— hence the big fall on Saturday night. The soles of my feet have been horizontal for the past twelve months and squeezing into those strappy little numbers gave them quite a fright.'

He'd crossed the room now and was standing not a foot away. Leah swallowed hard as he looked down at her. 'And the others?'

'The others?'

'You said there were three types.'

'Oh, yes. The misfits.' He didn't smile but it was there in his eyes. Beautiful eyes, Leah thought as her mouth carried on moving as she attempted to answer his questions. 'I was in the misfit group and there were quite a few of us, rattling around on the Greyhound bus with no real idea why we were here in the first place. We sort of stuck together.'

'Why *did* you come?' Cole asked, his eyes narrowing slightly as he stared at her thoughtfully, noticing the tiny nervous swallow she gave as he voiced his question.

'Well, Kathy was here.' Leah shrugged vaguely, not liking the direction the conversation was taking all of a sudden, not sure she was quite ready to open up to Cole. 'And work was getting a bit…' Her voice trailed off as she waited hopefully for Cole to break in, to give a knowing nod and a groan, but instead he waited for her to finish, staring back patiently as her eyes darted over his shoulder and around the room, anywhere other than at him. 'I just needed a break,' Leah said eventually, her eyes finally managing to meet his, but still he didn't move, just gazed down at her, and she knew she hadn't answered his question properly, knew Cole was waiting for her to elaborate.

'I'll tell you what you need,' Cole said finally, when it was clear Leah wasn't going to add to her response, a slow lazy smile spreading over his lips. Leah found herself clenching her fists to her sides, resisting a sudden urge to reach out and touch him.

'What?' Leah croaked, the single word strangling in her throat. Any minute now, she thought frantically, any minute now I'm going to kiss him. I'm going to move forward and do something really stupid...

'Bed.'

She nodded lamely. She'd been thinking exactly the same thing but not quite along the same lines.

'Do you want me to carry you?'

'I'll manage,' Leah said firmly, heading for the stairs as Cole picked up her backpack. 'Dr Crean said—'

'I know, I know, gentle exercise is good.'

He hovered with infinite patience as she slowly took the stairs. 'It's all very well for Dr Crean,' Leah grumbled as they came to the bend at the top and she stood for a moment, catching her breath, as Cole went on ahead, flicking on lights and opening the bathroom door.

'You're in here.' His hand moved to the handle of the door of the spare bedroom but he changed his mind, depositing her backpack at the door. Despite the blazing lights, it was as if they'd been plunged into darkness. The closeness, the gentle teasing had gone as quickly as if a light had been switched off and Cole reverted to the rather austere man she had met on the plane. 'I'll say goodnight, then.'

'Goodnight,' Leah called to his rapidly departing back, frowning at the sudden change in him. But as she opened the bedroom door, as she gingerly bent down and picked up her backpack and stepped inside she understood in an instant the sudden dive in atmosphere. Her eyes filling with tears, she stared around the room, a trembling hand shooting up to her lips as she took in the lemon walls, the stripy curtains, the teddy-filled border that lovingly lined the walls and, worst of all, the horrible gap in the corner where a cot should have been.

It wasn't just a spare room, an unused corner of the house, it was a nursery, a lovingly, beautifully decorated, painfully empty nursery. 'Oh, Cole.' Sinking onto the bed, she ached, literally ached to go to him. Her fingers toyed with the duvet cover on the hastily made bed and she knew it must have hurt like hell for him to come in here. It was like reading someone's diary and finding all the answers. Or, worse than that, Leah thought frantically as she undressed and pulled on her pyjamas, it was like being caught reading someone's diary and knowing they knew that you knew.

It couldn't go unacknowledged.

She simply couldn't just lie down as if she didn't care.

Taking as deep a breath as one could with a fractured rib, she walked out of her bedroom, padding along the hallway in bare feet and hesitating for a moment before knocking softly on his bedroom door.

'Cole.'

He didn't answer and neither did she expect him to. Pushing the door open, she stood for a moment, watching as he lay unmoving on the vast bed that was way too big for one, just staring at the ceiling. Never had anyone looked lonelier.

'I'm sorry.' Still he didn't look at her, just stared at the ceiling as he spoke. 'I should have said something earlier, I just didn't know how to. I took down all the mobiles and things last night and put away the soft toys but I couldn't get the border off. I didn't mean it to upset you.'

'It didn't,' Leah started, then changed her mind. 'Well, it did, but not for me. I'm upset for you.' Crossing the room, she sat on the edge of the bed, her eyes brimming with tears. She played with her fingers for a moment, concentrating on keeping the tremor out of her voice, knowing this was Cole's agony, not hers. 'Did your baby die in the accident as well?' Hearing his sharp intake of breath, Leah cringed for a moment. 'I'm sorry, I wasn't being nosy, it's just that Kathy said there had been an accident but she just never said you had a baby as well.'

'We didn't.' Frowning, she looked up, wincing at the pain etched on his face as he spoke. 'At least, not according to the death certificate. Heather was four months pregnant,' he explained. 'Apparently, that doesn't count.'

'Oh, but it does,' Leah breathed, watching as Cole stared fixedly at the ceiling.

'What happened?' she ventured tentatively, longing for some insight, to try somehow to help. 'Kathy said something about boating…' Her voice trailed off as he shook his head.

'Leave it, Leah,' he said in a low voice, which was so loaded with pain she felt the splash of a tear from her brimming eyes trickle down her cheek.

'Don't you want to talk about it?'

He shook his head and Leah didn't push. She, more than most, knew about keeping things in.

'I'm here if you change your mind.' Standing up, she hesitated for an instant. It seemed wrong, so wrong to just walk away, but she heeded the warning note in his voice, knowing it wasn't her place to push. Reluctantly she crossed the bedroom, wishing she had somehow handled things differently, wishing she could somehow have treated Cole as skilfully as she treated grieving relatives at work. But this wasn't a stranger in an interview room, this wasn't someone she'd probably never see again, this was the man she loved.

Loved.

The realisation stilled her, her hand clutching convulsively on the doorhandle as the sensible part of her mind demanded a retraction. She barely knew him, had never even kissed him, so how on earth could she think that she loved him?

'Don't go.' His voice was so low, so loaded with pain it was barely audible, but it reached deep within, more an extension of her own thoughts than an audible request. As if her own internal revelation had somehow triggered in him this response. With a tiny nod of understanding she crossed back to the bed, did what she would have done to any friend in pain, treated Cole the way she would have Kathy or Kara, and leant over to give him a hug.

But he wasn't just a friend.

As her arms tentatively embraced him, the innocence in her gesture was lost as she felt the rough scratch of his chin against her cheek, breathed in the heady scent of him, and just as she knew she should pull away, should pat his shoulder and walk off, his arm reached out and pulled her in, burying his face in her hair and breathing her in as if she was the life force he needed to go. She held him then not as a friend but as a woman.

'Just because I don't want to talk about it,' Cole rasped, 'it doesn't mean that I want you to go.'

She nodded her understanding, words unnecessary now as touch took over. And anyway, Leah realised, with an absence of the facts, there was nothing she could say, nothing she could possibly say to make it even a little bit better. So instead she held him, just staring into the darkness, and he held her, only moving to slip the duvet over them. It should have felt wrong, the fact they were sharing a bed, should have sent her into a spin, but it didn't.

Lying in his arms, holding onto each other, seemed the only right thing to do.

'Leah.'

Opening her eyes, she saw the grey shadows of

early morning being chased away by the promise of a new day dawning, the glints of sunlight filtering across the rumpled sheets, the deep cosy warmth of a bed and confidences if not shared then at least acknowledged. She stared back at him, not blinking, not wavering, his early morning arousal nudging the warm curve of her thigh. While last night would have been a comfort for all the wrong reasons, the cold light of day allowed for absolute clarity and she moved her lips to his, the kiss they'd never shared but had always been there transpiring now as she moved her lips slowly with his, their bodies warm, already aroused from a night in each other's arms, the soft touches already imparted long before this moment. Sliding nearer as his hand stroked her waist, moving slowly upwards as a lazy breast stirred into life under his touch and one of them groaned as his fingers found her swollen nipple but neither was sure who. It was as if their bodies were moving as one, their thoughts completely attuned as she moved his boxers down, feeling his impatient kick as he tossed them aside and she could finally hold him in her hands, feel the tumid length swelling at her touch. And it was Leah now wriggling out of her shorts as his hand crept over the soft warm cup of her bottom as she guided him towards her, parting her soft thighs to let him in.

'Leah.' His voice was thick with lust and from her own aroused state she knew it would have taken a supreme effort to slow things down to make sure, very sure, that this was what she wanted, and she answered even before he'd asked.

'I want you, Cole.'

'But you're in pain.'

A hand reached for his chest, followed by her lips as they nestled into the dark mat of hair. 'We're both in pain.'

Side on they faced each other, eyes wide open as they took the next step forward together. Mindful of her injuries, he entered her slowly, supporting her body with his arms, moving inside her gently, until then she groaned for more, urged him deeper, coiling her leg over him, pulling him closer, the heady elixir of his touch the sweetest antidote to her pain, kissing it better as only Cole could. The strength of her orgasm caught her unawares, creeping up slowly, a flickering pulse beating a distant drum as his thigh moved against hers, the salty taste of his chest sliding against her lips, his breath coming harder, then a low thundering moan as he swelled within her.

And suddenly she was there too, gasping as her body seemed to take on a mind of its own, coiling around him as her fingers gripped the taut muscles of his back, clinging on for dear life as everything rushed around her, a heady dizzy flush warming her face, parting her lips in shuddering ecstasy, spurring the last throes of their union to a dizzy breathlessness then slowly, slowly opening her eyes as the world gently breezed back in.

'Good morning.' He was smiling back at her, a secret delicious smile she had never seen, an intimate smile that caressed every inch of her spent body like a warm blanket in winter, and she searched his eyes for a hint of regret, contrition, doubt but there was none. She had to be sure, she knew, just knew, there had been no one since his wife and the fact couldn't go unacknowledged.

'Good morning,' she whispered, one small hand coming up to cup his cheek. 'Are you all right, Cole? I mean, I know this would have been—'

He didn't let her finish, capturing her hand with his and chasing away her doubts with a long lingering kiss. 'It was perfect.'

CHAPTER SIX

PERFECT just about summed up those first few weeks.

Oh, there were a couple of dicey moments, when Cole's in-laws rang and Leah picked up the phone without thinking and they growled at each other now and then, Cole refusing to believe she could possibly be well enough to clean the bath, that sort of thing. But they soon made up, the house small enough for the bedroom to always be near. For a while nothing got in the way and by the time the newlyweds hit England the euphoria in Kathy's voice when she heard the news seemed a touch belated, so natural was the relationship they'd slipped into.

'So you're living together!'

'No.' Leah grinned. 'Well, yes, I suppose we are, but I wouldn't exactly call it living together.' Cole slipped a glass of wine into her free hand and snapped his index finger and thumb at the phone in a nattering gesture as Kathy gossiped on.

'What would you call it, then?'

'Early days.' Leah smiled, winking at Cole. 'So don't go getting any ideas.'

But Kathy's head was full of them and by the time Leah came off the telephone the late night news was wrapping up.

'Have you chosen the bridesmaids?' Cole grinned, pulling her towards him as she plonked onto the sofa.

'Kathy has.' Yawning, Leah listened to the weather. Strange how much it mattered when you were cooped up inside. 'She said I could use her car. She's going to ring her mum and I can pick it up tomorrow.'

'It's too soon.' Thinking she'd misheard, Leah turned and gave him a quizzical look but from the set of his jaw she knew she'd hit a nerve. 'Anyway, you said yourself you haven't driven in this country.'

'Cole!' Leah let out an incredulous laugh. 'I live in London, for goodness' sake. I drive in London! What you guys call a traffic jam we call a traffic light so I think I can just about manage the suburbs of Melbourne. You even drive on the same side of the road!'

'I'm just saying that maybe it's too soon.' Flicking off the television, Cole stood up and stretched. 'I don't mind driving you when I'm home and I've got an account with the local taxi firm, I've told you that.'

'I know,' Leah responded through slightly gritted teeth. 'I'll ring them tomorrow and they can take me to pick up the car.' It wasn't a row exactly, but it was as if a warning light went off in her head. At first his over-protectiveness had been endearing, had flattered her even, but as Leah's strength had returned so too had her independence and she wasn't about to let things rest. 'I know what happened with Heather probably makes you…' Her voice trailed off, her hand reaching out to touch his. 'Nothing's going to happen to me.'

'Good.' Cole refused to be drawn but Leah pushed on anyway, her need for answers overriding her apprehension at broaching this most difficult subject. But it wasn't just answers Leah wanted. There was a need inside, a hunger almost to get to know Cole more deeply, to explore all the pieces of the jigsaw that made up this difficult, complicated man. As his hand pulled away, as Cole effectively ended the conversation and headed upstairs, still she couldn't let it rest.

'Actually, I don't know what happened to Heather,' Leah ventured as she padded up behind him, glad that she couldn't see his face as she followed his stiffening shoulders up the stairs, imagining the stern set of his jaw as she refused to let the subject go. 'I don't know, because you refuse to talk about it. But I'm assuming that's the real reason for you being a bit over-protective.' They were at the top of the stairs now and, swallowing hard, Leah dragged her eyes up to meet his. 'Why won't you talk to me about it, Cole?'

'We are talking.' Cole shrugged. 'Or rather you're talking and I'm being forced to listen. You were trying to tell me you needed more space.'

'That isn't what I'm saying,' Leah refuted, shaking her head in exasperation, appalled he couldn't see her point. 'I was trying to point out that I don't know what happened to Heather, that if you'd only open up a bit and tell me, then maybe I could understand why you—'

'She died,' Cole broke in, staring back at her unblinking, unwavering and refusing to give an inch. 'If you're waiting for me to curl up in the foetal position and bare my soul then you're in for a long wait.'

'I'm not,' Leah said. 'I just...' Pleading eyes

looked up at him. 'How can we not talk about it, Cole? Heather was, is, the biggest part of your life and you simply won't go there with me.'

His expression was unreadable in the shadows and his voice, when it came, was so clipped and measured she felt as if they might just as well have been back on the plane. 'What do you want from me, Leah?'

'The truth.'

'That's a bit rich, coming from you.' He watched as her eyes widened, watched as she opened her mouth to speak, but beat her to it. 'You're the one with all the secrets, Leah. You're the one who checked out of her world and drifted around for a year. You're the one "doesn't want to talk about it", so I think you of all people should understand that maybe I don't want to stand here and go through Heather's accident. You of all people should understand I don't want to rake up the worst time of my life just to satisfy your curiosity.'

If she'd looked up then Leah would have seen his face soften, would have seen the fire die in his eyes, but instead she focused somewhere on her big toe, somewhere on a piece of chipped nail varnish, biting hard on her bottom lip as she tried not to cry.

'Don't you think I've got questions?' Cole whispered softly, his fingers toying with the curtain of hair that shielded her eyes, pushing her long fringe behind her ear, as she still didn't look at him. 'That there're things I feel I ought to know?' When she didn't answer he pressed on, and even though his assumptions were wrong it was done with a gentleness that touched her, a tenderness that put to shame her less than tactful probing. 'But I sense you're not quite ready to go there and if that's the case, then that's the way it has to be. Leah, I can't bear the thought that your boyfriend did this to you. I lie here at night churning with hatred for a man I've never met and with a thousand things I want to ask you, but I know you'll tell me when you're ready and I'm asking you for the same. We're not in this for the short term, or at least I hope not?' The question in his voice deserved an answer and it was there in her eyes when finally she lifted her face to his. 'Surely there's time for all this later?'

Taking her hand, he led her to the bedroom, undressed her with infinite gentleness before lying down beside her, pulling her close into the crook of his arm which was the only place she wanted to be. And as their breathing evened out and the horrors of their first real row finally receded Leah was filled with an urge to put things right, to finally let Cole in.

'It wasn't my boyfriend.'

Her voice filled the still darkened room and she felt his arm tighten around her. She drew from his strength, drew from the infinite safeness of his embrace.

'It was a patient.'

'Oh, Leah,' Cole groaned. Rolling onto his side, he faced her, his arms still holding her, his eyes never leaving hers as, faltering every now and then, Leah took him through the worst night of her life, told him how not only had her rib cage been shattered by the terrible events that had unfolded but her confidence along with it. And watching Cole's reaction, Leah couldn't be sure who was hurting more as she bared her soul.

If she'd wanted sympathy, Leah got it.

If she wanted him to feel her pain then he did—tenfold.

He held her, loved her, somehow even protected her, walking through her memories alongside her, a retrospective rock to cling to as she finally let it out.

'That's why I left Emergency,' Leah finished, burying her face in his chest, her tears mingling with the dark mat of his hair. 'I just couldn't do it any more. As soon as the verdict came in, I handed in my notice. I figured a year away might help me forget what happened, put some of the fire back in my belly for nursing. I know it's stupid, I know there's only a minuscule chance of it happening again, but it still terrifies me…'

'It's over,' Cole said softly. 'It's over, Leah, and you've come through.'

'Have I?' Her eyes blinked up at him. 'Sometimes I think I'm over it then something happens, someone—'

'It's over, Leah.' His voice was firm, strong eyes holding hers as they clung to each other in the darkness. 'You're doing just fine.'

Maybe she was.

Lying there wrapped in his embrace, feeling him breathing in her ear, it was easy to feel safe, easy to glimpse the future with Cole standing strong beside her. Only as she drifted off to sleep, as Cole's arm slid down her shoulder, resting gently on the curve of her waist, did her eyes snap open as realisation suddenly hit.

She had told him of her pain, shared her deepest fears, her darkest secrets, yet she still knew nothing more about him.

CHAPTER SEVEN

'WHAT the hell do you think you're doing?'

Clinging to the edge of the pool, Leah chose to look at Cole's highly polished shoes rather than upwards, positive from the tone of his voice that Cole wasn't about to greet her with a smile.

'Swimming.'

'I can see that,' Cole responded, offering her his hand, which she reluctantly accepted, and hauling her out of the pool. 'The question, though, is, what the hell are you doing swimming with your type of injury?'

'I didn't think you'd be home for a while.'

'So this isn't the first time?'

Wrapping a towel around her, Leah still didn't look up and she didn't answer, just concentrated on drying herself as Cole stood there, waiting for a response.

'Leah?' Cole demanded, following her in as she tossed her hair and headed inside.

Leah sucked in her breath before turning angry eyes to Cole. 'You're right, Cole, this isn't the first time, and I didn't want to tell you because I knew you'd overreact. So instead I've been sneaking around like a schoolgirl smoking behind the bike sheds, hiding my bathers, which, the more I think about it, the more pathetic I realise it is. I'm not doing anything wrong. It's supposed to be good exercise for my lungs. I told you all of this after my last outpatient appointment. Dr Crean said—'

'Oh, what would he know?' Cole broke in, incensed, and Leah let out an incredulous laugh.

'Quite a bit, I hope! He's a thoracic surgeon, for heaven's sake,' Leah responded hotly, and Cole at least had the grace to look a bit embarrassed. 'He also said that I'm ready to go back to work.'

'Which is immaterial,' Cole said through white lips, 'given the fact that you don't have a job.'

'Wrong.' Picking up the newspaper from the coffee-table, she handed it to him, watching as he read it, a muscle pounding in his cheek. 'I start on Friday evening.'

'Bar work?'

She heard the derisive tone in his voice and instantly she retaliated. 'What? Is it beneath an emergency consultant to be seen with a barmaid?'

'Don't make me out to be a snob here, Leah.'

'You turned your nose up when I told you what I did on the plane.' Despite him shaking his head she carried on talking. 'And you're turning up your nose now.'

'I was turning up my nose at your extra-curricular activities, Leah, not your job.' He stared at the paper for a moment before flinging it down. 'It's a bar, Leah. Do you really think they're going to care that you're getting over a pneumothorax?'

'I'm over it, Cole.'

'No, Leah, you're not. And the last thing you need to be doing is lugging kegs of beer around and collecting glasses in a room full of smoke. I've said I don't need rent and you told me your parents had sent you some money.'

'Cole.' Her voice was very steady, very calm, despite the fury welling inside her, a thousand tiny niggles over the past couple of weeks all aligning, the off-the-cuff remarks that had been dusted under the carpet surfacing now, pinging into her mind with appalling clarity and culminating in this one dark moment. 'My parents' idea of a living wage and my idea tend to differ.' He opened his mouth to argue and she knew, just knew, he was about to offer her money, but money wasn't the problem here, or at least not all of it. 'I don't want money from you, Cole, I want to earn my own. I'm twenty-nine years old, nearly thirty actually, and I'm not about to start lining up for pocket money from you or from anyone. If I need some cash then I'll go and earn it. Are you such a chauvinist you don't think women should work?'

'Don't be ridiculous.' He shook his head fiercely. 'Heather…' Swallowing hard, he stiffened, clenching his fists by his side as Leah stared wide-eyed, waiting for him to continue.

'Heather worked, then?' Leah pushed, but Cole didn't answer. 'What did she do?'

'Leave it, Leah,' Cole warned, but Leah had had enough of skirting around the edges. Heather was a massive part of Cole's life and needed to be discussed.

'Why?' Leah asked simply. 'You barely speak about her, yet surely you must want to. What are you so afraid of?'

He gave a scoffing laugh. 'I'm not afraid of anything.'

'I don't believe you, Cole.' She was shivering now, her skin still damp from the pool, her hair wet and cold and dripping down her back. 'Heather's a no-go area where we're concerned.'

'She isn't,' Cole answered irritably, but Leah begged to differ.

'You won't even tell me what she did for a living.'

He blinked back at her, his face slipping into impassive, his voice annoyingly detached, and Leah knew despite his answer that he was shutting her out.

'She was a fitness instructor.' Cole shrugged. 'A personal trainer. She ran a business from home—hence the lap pool, hence the massive blender in the kitchen so Heather could whip up her fruit smoothies. So, you see, I can talk about her. And if I'm afraid of anything it's coming home and finding you face down in the pool because you developed chest pain and couldn't get to the edge in time, which is actually quite a valid concern given what you've been through.' Pulling a rug from the sofa, he wrapped it around her. 'That and catching your death of cold, of course.'

Sitting down on the edge of the sofa, Leah ran a slightly trembling hand through her damp hair, turning her chlorine-shot eyes to his. 'I'm not a doll, Cole. I'm not some fragile porcelain doll that's going to shatter.'

The fight seemed to go out of him then. Slowly he replaced the newspaper on the coffee-table but she didn't look up. She could hear his ragged breathing, hear the ticking of the clock on the mantelpiece, but she didn't say anything. It was up to Cole to make the next move.

'I'm sorry,' he started as Leah sat there unmoved. 'I know I can be a bit overbearing…'

'A bit?'

'A lot,' Cole admitted. 'I just can't bear the thought of anything happening to you. I know you play it down but I was there, Leah. You nearly died that night…'

'But I didn't.'

He nodded, and then ran a weary hand across his chin. 'They're short-staffed in Emergency.' He looked up as she blinked back at him. 'They need some nurses. Why don't I ask Fay, she's the unit manager, if there's a spot there for you? If you join the nursing bank you can do casual shifts in Emergency.'

When she didn't answer he pressed right on. 'Look I've told you over and over to stop worrying about money, Leah, but I can understand that you want to earn some of your own. I'm not that much of a chauvinist and apparently the money's pretty good for casual staff. Perhaps more to the point, unlike working in a bar, there's a no-lift policy in the department.' He saw the confusion in her eyes and explained further. 'The nurses don't lift, they use slide mats or hoists so you wouldn't strain yourself…'

She only half listened as he carried on, reeling off the practicalities, the merits of going back, and though it all made perfect sense, though he'd clearly thought this through, Leah felt fury well within her, shaken to the core at his callousness, outraged at his insensitivity. 'I thought you understood.' Chewing the skin around her nail, hurt, confused eyes dragged up to his. 'I told you what happened to me, Cole. I thought you'd at least—'

'You just said you didn't want to be treated like a doll, Leah,' Cole pointed out.

'I don't,' Leah responded fiercely, 'but that doesn't mean I want to be thrown in at the deep end.'

'As opposed to jumping in?' Cole gestured to the pool outside. 'That was reckless, Leah, but this makes sense.'

'Not to me.' Her voice caught in her throat. 'I don't think I'm ready, Cole '

He joined her on the sofa and she ached for him to pull her in, to wrap her in his arms and tell her she was right, that of course it was too soon. Instead, he sat there, letting out a long slow breath before finally he turned to face her.

'I'll be there for you,' Cole said gently but firmly. 'Do you want me to ask?'

Leah knew it was now or never and if she was going to go back to nursing now was surely the time. And perhaps more pointedly, she needed the money. Kara, for all her initial promises, hadn't been exactly forthcoming in coughing up the rent and a couple of shifts in Emergency would earn more dollars than a week of working in a bar for minimum wages. She was more than qualified after all. Her résumé along with her references, were there with her passport and air ticket. She'd even got her Australian registration just in case the urge had taken her all of a sudden.

'Leah?' The question in his voice demanded an answer.

'That would be great.' She forced a watery smile. 'Do you want me to follow up with a call this afternoon to the unit manager?'

'It would probably be better if Fay rings you,' Cole suggested, 'when she's got a quiet moment. Do you have a copy of your résumé I could give to her?'

Leah nodded. Heading upstairs, she pulled out her papers with shaking hands as Cole came into the bedroom behind her. 'There's my registration certificate as well and a couple of references.'

'You won't mind?' Cole flicked through the first page of her résumé raising an approving eyebrow. 'Working as an RN when you're used to being in charge?'

'I won't mind a bit.' Cole missed the dry note to her voice. 'Give me a call when you've spoken to Fay.'

As he kissed her goodbye and made to go, Leah stalled at the last hurdle, desperate to grab her papers, to put an end to whatever they were starting. 'Maybe we should think about this,' Leah called to his departing back. 'It might not work.' She was tossing up excuses now, trying to form an escape route—anything rather than face going back. 'I mean, living together and working together are two different things. What if there's a problem at work, what if I do something wrong and you have to haul me out—?'

'I don't *haul* out my staff, as you so eloquently put it,' Cole responded in a slightly superior tone as he came back over to her. 'If there's a problem I discuss it rationally and listen to both sides before making a decision.'

'Silly me for thinking otherwise!' Leah blinked, a smile twisting her strained lips as Cole even had the decency to look uncomfortable. 'So it's only at home you jackboot about?'

Her humour only lasted a moment. Screwing her eyes closed, she balled her fists against her temples, sucking in her breath as the roller-coaster ride started again.

'You can do this, Leah.' His hand found hers then. Hot and strong, he gripped her cold fingers all wrinkled from the pool and held them tight. 'I'll be right there beside you.'

You'll always be guaranteed a job, people will always need nurses.

How many times had she heard that? Pulling into the staff car park Leah seemed to have taken for ever to find, she sat for a moment staring at the emergency department ahead of her—an ambulance pulling up in a bay, the hub of activity outside, people chatting into mobiles, grabbing a smoke or a coffee. Apart from the sun, apart from the sight of male nurses in shorts, she could just as well have been back in London. For days she'd pored over the local papers, ringing up café after café, bar after bar before landing a questionable offer of eight, maybe ten hours a week, whereas Cole had seemingly barely left the house before the nurse supervisor had called, inviting her to come in for an informal chat and tour of the department.

Nurses *were* always needed and add a trauma and ICU certificate to the equation and the world was your oyster.

She stepped out of the car and walked purposefully over to the unit, uncomfortable in her new uniform. Hardly a uniform really, Leah thought, looking down. Used to wearing a dress and belt for work, it felt strange to be dressed in culottes and a white polo shirt, her new name tag hanging round her neck.

'Don't lose it,' Fay had warned, when she had taken Leah down to Security to get her photo taken. 'And if you do, alert Security straight away so they can cancel it.'

Fay, the unit manager, was as nice as she had been at the interview, friendly and welcoming, but Leah knew from the short time they had spent together that nothing would get past those shrewd eyes of hers and she was grateful for that fact, glad to be just a number on her first day back.

'Now, ideally I'd have liked to pair you up with someone,' Fay chattered as she whizzed Leah through the department, 'but with the staff shortages we really can't manage it. Now, there's no need to feel shy, half the staff on duty are either agency or bank and on their first shift here.' Catching Leah's wry grin, Fay stopped walking for a moment. 'Does that sound familiar?'

'Just a bit,' Leah agreed. 'It's the same in England.'

'It's the same the world over, no doubt,' Fay groaned. 'At least you've actually worked in Emergency. You were a charge nurse there, weren't you?'

Leah smiled as she nodded. 'Don't let that stop you telling me what to do.'

'Good girl.' Fay gave a grateful nod. 'Now, at anyone time we've got two junior doctors on. They can see and advise treatment, but referral and discharge has to be done by either a registrar or a consultant, and at any given time we've got one in the department—or restroom or canteen,' Fay added with a low laugh. Then suddenly she seemed to change her mind and looked over at Leah with an apologetic smile. 'Sorry, I forgot. You're Cole's girlfriend, aren't you?'

Fay's reservation didn't come as any surprise. Leah had actually been wondering how to address the fact she was living with Cole, unsure whether or not Cole was quite ready to go public. But it would seem Cole didn't have a problem with the world and his wife realising they were actually an item.

'Forget that, too.' Leah grinned to Fay. 'Like I said before, don't let that little fact stop you telling me what to do.'

'Good girl,' Fay said again. 'There's no room for egos here. Well, now we've at least got that out of the way we can get down to business. I've put you down for cots—the paediatric area,' she explained. 'There are eight general beds comprising four cots and four trolleys. There's a television and video as well and, believe me, by the time the shift's over you'll know every Wiggles' song off by heart!' Pushing open a door, Leah peered in, taking in the vital equipment lining the walls, a resuscitation cot in the corner with a large red crash trolley pushed up against the wall. 'This is the paediatric resus area, though if a child's that sick generally we'll move them straight up to the main resus. Are you happy to go in there if we need a hand?'

Leah nodded. Resus didn't unnerve her in the least. Unconscious patients she could deal with, it was the wide-awake arguing type she had a problem with!

'Now, you've got a grad nurse with you—Tara. It's her first week in Emergency but she's pretty on the ball. Sort out your coffee-breaks between the two of you and, like I said, if you need anything just call.'

'Do I need keys or anything,' Leah asked as Fay made to go, 'for the drug cupboard?'

'Round your neck.' Coming over, Fay held up the swipe card that had got Leah into the car park. 'That will get you into the drug cupboard but if it's controlled drugs you need you'll have to come and get the keys from me.'

It wasn't exactly the most thorough of tours but it would have to do. Thankfully, because the department hadn't been so busy then, Fay had shown her around a touch more thoroughly during her interview, so at least Leah had a handle on most things.

'Leah!' The smiling face coming out from behind a curtain was mercifully familiar.

'Tara.' The warmth in Leah's voice was genuine. Tara had not only been kind to her when she had been a patient but an efficient and thorough nurse as well. It made the whole afternoon a touch less daunting knowing she would be working with someone so competent. 'It's good to see you again.'

'It's good to see you.' Tara gave a slight grimace. 'Actually, it's really good.' She lowered her voice and

Leah knew the small talk was over and it was straight down to business. 'I've got a two-year-old in here and the mum just found him chewing on this.' Tara held up a half-empty blister packet of paracetamol. 'She's almost beside herself. I told Fay and she didn't seem too concerned. She said to tell the mother that the doctor might be a while but when I said that the mother just went off, said she'd read in the newspaper that even a few paracetamol can be fatal and that the doctor had to come and see her now. She's nearly beside herself.'

Leah gave a wry smile. Fay had been right—emergency medicine really was the same the world over. Gesturing for Tara to follow her, Leah had a brief look at the casualty card before pulling open the curtain and stepping inside the cubicle. 'Mrs Thomsen, my name's Leah.'

Mrs Thomsen clearly didn't care what Leah's name was. She was trying to push a dummy into a fretful baby while stopping her hyperactive two-year-old from climbing over the cot sides. Leah could feel the tension before the curtain had even stopped flapping. 'You think that Riley might have taken some paracetamol.'

'You tell me.' Mrs Thomsen turned, teary bloodshot eyes meeting Leah's. 'I walked into the bathroom and he's holding onto a half-empty packet and now I've got everyone asking me how many were in the packet before I found him.

'How many were in the packet?' Mrs Thomsen repeated herself, her voice rising with each and every word. 'How on earth would I know? I don't know how he got them in the first place. I keep all the medicines locked up, all of them,' she reiterated. 'I know you don't believe me, that you probably think I just leave them lying about, but I don't. I'm always so careful, I just can't believe I'm here. And nobody's doing anything. I read in the paper....' Picking up her wailing infant she tried to drag her toddler down from the cot side and Leah's heart went out to her, first-day nerves instantly forgotten as she addressed her patient.

'Mrs Thomsen,' Leah started. 'Or Jan, if you don't mind me calling you that?'

A brief shrug was her only answer, but Leah pressed on anyway. 'Paracetamol is extremely dangerous and you were right to bring Riley straight in.' Pulling down the cot sides, Leah picked up the hyperactive bundle, deliberately ignoring his jammy fingers, which instantly reached for her name badge and stethoscope, allowing Jan to concentrate on her baby. 'Does she need a feed?' Leah asked, and Jan gave a small nod. 'Do you need a bottle?'

'I'm breastfeeding,' Jan snapped, but Leah remained unfazed even though Riley was exploring her pockets now.

'Go ahead.' She politely played with Riley as Jan settled her infant and once some sort of order was restored Leah carried on talking. 'Like I said, it was very sensible of you to bring Riley to Emergency. Paracetamol can be extremely dangerous, and you're right—even a few tablets can be serious in children as young as Riley. The trouble is, you found Riley chewing on the packet an hour ago...' She watched as Jan gave a hesitant nod. 'Paracetamol takes a while to be absorbed. If we take Riley's blood now, even if he has taken some, it will only show a trace, which would be misleading. We have to wait four to six hours after ingestion to take the bloods.'

'But if he has taken them, won't it be doing damage now?' Jan asked. 'Shouldn't you pump his stomach just in case?'

'A few years ago we would have.' Leah nodded. 'Just in case, as you said. But it's been shown to be ineffective.' Taking the half-empty blister pack from Tara, who was watching quietly, Leah handed it to Riley. 'In all probability Riley hasn't taken any.'

'How do you know?' Jan asked, but the hysteria had gone from her voice, Leah's quiet, assured tones calming the tension. 'How can you be sure?'

'I can't be sure, but two-year-olds generally don't have the fine motor skills needed to push a tablet out of the blister pack.' They looked down as Riley, gummy and smiling, played with the empty blister pack and Jan finally seemed to relax. 'The risk is that there were a couple lying around, unaccounted for, that perhaps the pack was half-open. Where two-year-olds are concerned you can never really be sure. So I'm afraid you're in for a horrible long day, hanging around waiting for a blood test, then another few hours waiting for the result, only to be told that Riley hasn't taken any anyway.'

'I don't mind that,' Jan said, a smile finally breaking out on her strained face, 'just as long as he's all right.'

'I'm sure he will be,' Leah said firmly. 'But if the

blood test does show that he's taken too much, then we'll be straight onto it. There's an antidote that can be given but it has to be administered within a strict timeframe, so you really were right to bring Riley in. Accidents happen, Jan. This wasn't anyone's fault.' Leah was making to go now, happy the situation was under control and that Jan understood the reason for the delay.

'Try telling that to my husband.' Something in her voice stilled Leah, a slightly weary, pensive note that Leah, no matter how busy, couldn't ignore.

'Are things a bit tough at home?'

'A bit?' Jan's brimming eyes spilled over. Tara relieved Leah of Riley and Leah pulled up a chair.

'Can Riley eat?' Tara asked. 'There are some sandwiches in the fridge and I could put a video on for him.'

'Good idea,' Leah answered gratefully, glad of Tara's tact, knowing it would be easier for Jan to open up without an audience and her two-year-old son watching. 'Is there anyone waiting?'

Tara peered outside and shook her head. 'I'll call if I need you.'

Once they were alone, Leah took a couple of tissues from the box on the shelf and handed them to Jan, who wept quietly for a moment before talking.

'I feel so stupid,' she started. 'Rick's going to be furious.'

'Rick's your husband?' Leah checked, and Jan nodded miserably. 'Like I said before, Jan, it was an accident, we see this sort of thing all the time.'

'That's no excuse, though, is it? Medications

should be locked up—everyone knows that. I'm always so careful. I just don't know what's wrong with me lately.' She gave a quick shake of her head and, stuffing the tissues into her pocket, she forced a brave smile. The baby had finished feeding now and Jan stood up, laying the infant down in the cot reserved for Riley. Leah helped her to pull up the heavy metal cot side.

'I'm being ridiculous, overreacting,' Jan said as firmly as she could, trying to put on a brave face. 'I just got such a fright when I found him with the tablet pack but I'll be fine now. You get on, sister. I'm sure you've got a hundred things to do without listening to my problems.'

'It's my job to listen,' Leah said gently, not moving an inch. 'And sometimes talking about things can help. Put things into perspective a bit.' She watched as Jan, after a moment's hesitation, sat back down and gazed over at her sleeping baby before pulling the tissues back out.

'Everything's such a mess...'

'Mrs Thomsen! What's been happening today?'

As nice as it was to see Cole, as the curtain was pulled open, Leah groaned inwardly at his appalling timing, sure that Jan had been just about to open up to her. But this was an emergency department, Leah reminded herself, handing over the casualty card and carrying on with the next patient, hoping Cole wasn't about to deliver Jan a stern lecture on the perils of not keeping medication locked up. Debating whether to call Cole out and ask him to go a little bit easy on the woman, Leah gave herself a mental shake. It wasn't her place to tell Cole his job. Anyway, he was a consultant which would mean a query paracetamol overdose in a two-year-old would barely merit a glance, let alone an in-depth consultation.

Or so she thought! It came as a pleasant surprise when Cole tapped her on the shoulder a couple of hours later.

'Can you hold Riley while I take some blood? I'm going to suggest Mum goes and grabs a coffee while we do it—she's still a bit on edge.'

'Sure.'

'How are you finding things?' Cole asked as they walked towards the treatment room.

'Surprisingly good. It's pretty much the same as what I'm used to, although the patients here are crook instead of sick and there's a few different drug names to get used to.'

'You're doing great,' Cole said warmly. They were at the treatment room now and Cole pulled her to one side, before they stepped inside, adopting a slightly more formal tone. 'It would seem the paracetamol belongs to Mr Thomsen.'

Leah gave a frown as Cole thrust a card under her nose, her mind stuck in obs room two where a child had fallen off his cycle, his scream filling the room as Leah attempted to take Tara through the Glasgow coma scale observation chart. 'He's away interstate a lot on business.'

'You've lost me,' Leah admitted.

'Mr Thomsen had a headache when he was on a business trip in Perth and bought some paracetamol,' Cole explained patiently. 'He took a couple then zipped the pack into the front of his toiletry bag and completely forgot about it. Naturally Jan didn't think to check when she unpacked his case, just took out the toiletries and put the bag back in the bathroom cupboard hence Riley rummaging through the cupboard and finding them. It was a complete accident that could happen to anyone, and if it's anyone's fault then I'd say it was more Mr Thomsen's.'

'But?' Leah asked, cutting to the chase, knowing there would be one.

'Jan's pretty close to the edge. We've had a long chat and it would seem her husband's been away an awful lot on business recently and when he comes home he seems to expect the house to be perfect, everything running smoothly, which is a pretty tough task given that there's a five-year-old and six-year-old at school as well as the two little ones.'

'Do you think she's got postnatal depression?' Leah asked, tossing up possibilities and enjoying the discussion. Emergency was a busy place, patients came and went, but one of the nicer parts of the job was delving into people's lives, going that extra mile to help a relative stranger. It made the work so much more interesting, so much more personal, and she was quietly pleased that Cole seemed to feel the same. Many doctors would have dealt with facts to hand, written up Riley for a blood test and carried right on, but Cole had taken things further, treated not only the patient but his family too. It was as refreshing as it was welcome. 'I mean, the baby's only a few months old and she's got a two-year-old to deal with as well.'

'She could have,' Cole agreed, 'but I'd say that

exhaustion is a more probable diagnosis and unfortunately that isn't going to improve—at least not in
the short term,' Cole added with a dry edge to his
voice. 'I've just run a pregnancy test on Jan and guess
what?'

Leah gave a low groan as Cole let out a rueful
laugh. 'I'm going to call her GP and ask her to follow
things up, not just with the pregnancy. I think Jan
needs a bit of support at the moment.'

'Do you want me to give the social worker a ring?'
Leah asked. 'I don't know if that's how it's done here,
but in England…'

'Done.' Cole smiled. 'Jasmine's going to come
down in the next half hour or so. I told her there
wasn't a huge rush—until Riley's blood results come
back, Mrs Thomsen won't be going anywhere. Mind
you, personally I don't think it's Jan she needs to be
talking to. I'd say Mr Thomsen needs pulling to one
side.'

'Oh, I don't know.' Leah grinned. 'She might be
able to offer some contraceptive advice.'

He stalked into the treatment room with barely a
backward glance, and Leah was infinitely grateful for
his apparent indifference to her. Working with your
lover wasn't the greatest scenario at the best of times
and since her interview endless problems they could
have faced working together, had played on her mind,
but thankfully none had come to fruition. Cole had
set the tone, and to the world they would seem like
normal working colleagues.

Almost.

Practically wrestling Riley to the floor, Fay had

come in to help and passed the tubes as Cole took the blood.

'Swab,' Cole barked, slipping the needle out.

Leah loosened her grip.

'Have you got some tape?' Fay asked pushing down on the swab as she patted her pockets.

'Ask Leah,' Cole said, syringing the blood into a couple of tubes. 'I'm sure she'll have some stashed away!'

'I was starting to get worried.'

Leah plonked down on the sofa and kicked off her shoes, letting out a grateful sigh as Cole handed her a welcome glass of wine. Lord, he looked divine, even though she'd seen him all afternoon at work. Out of his suit he looked infinitely more casual, more approachable, more the Cole she adored.

'Why were you worried?' Leah asked. 'My shift didn't end till nine.' Glancing down at her watch, she saw it edging past ten and realised how long she'd actually been. 'Fay handed me the off-duty,' she said in an almost shy voice, not wanting to blow her own trumpet. 'She was pretty pleased with how my first day went so she gave me my pick of the shifts that need filling.'

'You were great,' Cole said enthusiastically, but Leah shook her head.

'I was *OK*,' she corrected, blushing as she did so, unable to accept his compliment. '*Great* is what I used to be in London—at least I knew what I was doing there! I seem to have spent half the day asking where things were kept and the other half being shown the mistakes I'd made. You're just biased.'

'Fay's not, though,' Cole pointed out. 'If anything, she had her reservations about you working there in the first place, so the fact she's given you first pick of the shifts says a lot.' He gave a slight grimace. 'I think she was worried we'd be making smouldering eyes at each other over the drug trolley.'

'I was worried about that too,' Leah admitted, grinning as she took a sip of her drink. 'Not the smouldering-eyes bit, I know we're both a bit more professional than that, but I've never worked with someone I've been going out with, and I wasn't sure how I'd find it.'

'It was OK, though, wasn't it?' Cole asked thoughtfully, and Leah nodded.

'It was nice having you there. I was nervous enough already and you being there really helped. Riley finally went home,' she added. 'It turns out he hadn't taken any paracetamol after all.'

'So poor Jan wasted an entire day in Emergency. The little monster.'

'I don't think it was a waste.' Leah smiled, remembering how good Cole had been with the woman.

Watching Cole at work had been a revelation in itself. Although formal and slightly austere at times, there was still an air of approachability about him and Leah had marvelled at the way he ran the busy department, taking time to listen to each and every patient, no matter how big or small their injury. And, more intriguingly, the respect he commanded from his colleagues wasn't merely related to his status, like so many consultants Leah had worked with, but more a genuine admiration for his undoubted skills and the way he effortlessly imparted his knowledge.

Far from her initial doubts, working alongside Cole had only served to make her want him more.

'I think in the scheme of things Jan will end up being glad today actually happened. Hopefully she'll get a bit of help now.'

'And hopefully we're not going to talk shop all the time,' Cole said in a low voice, taking the glass of wine from her and fixing her with a look that had Leah's insides flipping over. 'Work's work and home's…' His fingers were fiddling with her name tag, pulling at the cord, and it pulled open easily. Security had promised it would ping apart if an angry patient grabbed hold of it, but this wasn't an angry patient, this was Cole, and he was working his way down the buttons of her polo shirt now. 'Could this be home, Leah?'

She heard the question in his voice, knew the magnitude of what he was asking, but for a second her mind flashed to the other side of the world, to her family, her flat, her career and a life left at short notice, then back again to the man gazing at her with love blazing in his eyes, a man she could truly love if only he would let her.

'It could be.' Her hand reached out to his cheek, capturing the rough scratch of his jaw against her trembling hand, trying to ignore the massive *if* that seemed to hang over them.

'Could be?'

Her eyes drifted to the mantelpiece, to his wedding

photo, to a carefree man she'd barely glimpsed. And even though patience was a virtue and all that, even though he'd promised that in the fullness of time he would all be hers, she wanted him now, wanted each and every part of him.

'I love you, Cole,' Leah said, honesty resonating in her voice. 'But sometimes I feel as if I barely know you.'

For an age he stared at her, for an age she waited for some sort of response, some sort of answer, but instead of talking he moved in closer, his lips finding hers, chasing away her doubts, her questions, silencing her fears as she kissed him back harder, deeper, longer, the arousal he so easily instigated flicking on like a light switch, his touch, his smell, his taste the eternal trigger. He was pushing her back on the cushions now, the weight of his torso on hers unfamiliar after the gentleness of the previous weeks, unfamiliar but divine. She could feel the hardness of his arousal against her thigh, a bubble of moisture welling between her legs, and the questions that had taunted her flew out of the window as she arched her body towards him.

'I should have a shower,' Leah gasped but very half-heartedly.

'You should eat something,' Cole pointed out with just about as much enthusiasm.

Five minutes ago Leah would have agreed with him, but any pangs of hunger melted into oblivion as he slipped her shirt over her head and the zipper on the side of her culottes came under attack. 'Fay had every right to be worried.' Her culottes were on the floor now and he sat her up slowly. Lowering himself onto the floor, he ran an appreciative hand along the hollows of her waist. And she should have felt stupid, the lights blazing, Cole fully dressed, but something in his eyes told her she was beautiful. Wearing nothing but her undies and a seductive smile, she wriggled in anticipation as Cole slid her panties down before unclasping her bra, letting out a low moan of approval as her nipples stood rigid to attention, swelling further if that were possible as his fingers worked their magic, his tongue flicking them into frenzied life, stopping with a teasing annoyance every now and then as he spoke. 'If she had any idea the self-control I've had to muster all day, she'd never have let you near the off-duty.'

'You hid it amazingly well!' Her voice was coming out in small gasps now, the conversation taking place no indicator of the sensual foreplay taking place. 'You barely gave me a glance.'

Cole was undressing now, Cole pulling off his T-shirt and shorts, and she felt her breath catch in her throat as she gazed down at him kneeling before her as she wriggled back on the sofa, his fingers working their magic now on the nub of her clitoris.

'I was watching.' His voice was thick with lust now, his eyes blazing with desire as he reached for the peach of her buttocks, pulling them to the edge of the sofa before diving his swollen length into her. There was no question of holding back, no question of it being too soon. The foreplay had started this morning, the new sights, new sensations she had been experiencing all day, and the one constant had been

Cole. As he moved deeper within she coiled her legs around him, her bottom lifting off the sofa as his strong arms cradled her back and forth. 'I've been wanting to do this all day.' Burying his face in her splendid bosom, capturing her nipples in his cool mouth as she arched her back, her hands gripping his dark hair in spasm as she urged him deeper, talk running out now as their bodies spoke for themselves, the heady rush of her climax the sweetest homecoming of them all.

'All day,' he whispered as he held her close and the world slowly came back into focus.

They never did finish that talk, she never did have that shower, but a long bath run by Cole sufficed very nicely and later, much later they lay in bed, eating pizza from the box, still revelling in their post-coital bliss, still revelling in the magic of having found each other and trying to ignore the problems that surely lay ahead.

CHAPTER EIGHT

'IF A doctor doesn't come in here and see my daughter now, I'll go and find one and drag him in here myself!'

The angry tones coming from behind the curtain had the hairs rising on the back of Leah's neck. Casting a nervous look around, she willed a security guard to appear or for Fay to suddenly come over and tell her not to worry, that she'd deal with this.

But there was no one and Leah knew that her moment of truth had come—everyone was stuck in Resus with a multi-trauma and Security were busy ensuring the ambulance bay was clear for the next screeching ambulance that was due to arrive at any moment.

Oh, in the few weeks she'd been back in nursing she'd seen Melbourne Central busy, had even dealt with a couple of rather agitated patients, but they didn't compare to the furious shouts coming from behind the curtain and busy didn't come close to describing the emergency department this afternoon. The hot sultry weather seemed to be finally breaking and the highly charged skies threatening to storm matched the tense atmosphere in the department as they received the casualties from a four-car pile-up and the waiting room rumbled with dissatisfaction at

116

the appalling long wait and the fact the coffee-machine had finally given up the ghost.

'Leah?' Red-faced and clearly upset, Tara came out from behind the curtain and Leah kicked herself for her indecision, her hesitancy to help, as the young grad nurse came over. She was the RN after all. It should be she herself dealing with this, showing Tara how to handle anxious relatives, and instead she was pretending she hadn't noticed!

'I've got a one-year-old with gastro. The father brought her up last night and she was seen and discharged. Apparently they gave them some electrolyte replacement sachets for the little girl to take but she doesn't like the taste and she's been refusing to drink it. They've been giving her water and apple juice but she just keeps vomiting. The dad's really angry, he wants a doctor to come now, and frankly I can see why. The little girl doesn't look very well at all. If I were her mother I'd be pretty upset.'

Leah read through the card. Yesterday's admission notes were neatly clipped to it and from what Leah could see the child hadn't been particularly unwell last night, but with gastro things could unfortunately change very quickly. Taking a deep breath, Leah tried to ignore the angry noises coming from behind the curtain as she stepped inside.

'I don't want another nurse!' a young man roared as Leah came over. 'My daughter needs a doctor.'

'Mr Anderson.' Leah headed straight for the cot and looked at the little girl who lay spent and exhausted, barely looking up as Leah pulled down the cot sides and smiled gently at the babe. 'I'm the nurse in charge of cots this afternoon. The doctors are all in treating patients from a serious motor accident at the moment, so I'm going to have a look at your daughter and if needed I'll get someone in here straight away.'

'If needed!' Mr Anderson scoffed. 'Look at her! She must have been sick fifty times since we left here and all you lot can do is give her some drinks she can't even manage and tell us to keep bloody persevering.'

Despite her nerves Leah could more than understand Mr Anderson's agitation. This little girl was sick indeed. Her eyes were sunk in her head and, giving her skin a gentle pinch to check its turgor, Leah knew she was woefully dehydrated. Mr Anderson had every right to be anxious, and no doubt he was exhausted from lack of sleep as well. 'Tara, can you go and get a doctor please?' Leah said as she hastily examined the child.

'I've tried. They're busy in Resus, and the paediatricians are there with a head injury as well.'

'Tell one of the registrars or consultants to come now,' Leah said, widening her eyes and hoping Tara could read the urgency in them. 'Mr Anderson, I'm going to move Jessica to another area,' Leah said calmly, 'where we can give her some more help. A doctor will be here soon.'

Picking up the limp infant, Leah made her way swiftly into the paediatric resuscitation area. As Fay had pointed out on her first day, generally sick children were moved to the main resus area but, given that it was already full, for now at least that wasn't an option. Anyway, Leah realised as she laid the little girl down on the flat, hard resus bed, it wasn't the ideal place for an anxious family.

Slipping an oxygen mask over Jessica's face, Leah undressed her quickly then wrapped a tourniquet around the child's wrist in an attempt to bring up her veins. But she was on the verge of collapse, making her veins difficult to find, and Leah slapped the pale skin to bring them to the surface.

'What the hell are you doing?' Mr Anderson roared as Leah missed at her first attempt to get a needle in. 'Will you get someone in here who knows what to do?'

Taping a wad of cotton wool in place, Leah moved the tourniquet down and slapped at Jessica's hand before talking, trying to keep her voice as calm as possible. 'Mr Anderson, Jessica is very dehydrated, that's why her veins are so difficult to find. Once we get a needle in we can give her some fluid.' A thin blue vein was coming up now. Rubbing it with alcohol, Leah tried to keep her hand from shaking as Mr Anderson stood over her, watching her every move. Leah knew if she missed this time he was likely to explode, but his threatening stance wasn't exactly helping matters!

'Mr Anderson.' Sweat was beading on her brow now and, casting an anxious look up, she willed someone to appear at the door, but knew deep down she was on her own. 'I know how worried you are, Jessica is sick. Now, I need you to go around the other side of the bed.'

'I'm not going anywhere,' he roared, and Leah fixed him with a firm stare.

'Go around the other side of the bed,' she repeated measuredly, 'and hold onto your daughter so that if she jumps when I put the needle in, you can steady her. I don't want to get an IV line into her only to have her move and pull it out. I need your help here, Mr Anderson.'

Finally and to Leah's infinite relief he gave a brief, very short nod and Leah let out a small sigh as he moved around the other side and cradled his daughter.

'It's in,' Leah said, breathing a sigh of relief as she taped it firmly in place and flushed the line. 'Right, I'm going to run some IV fluids through a line and as soon as the doctor comes we can get...' Her voice trailed off as Tara arrived minus a doctor, and Leah knew with a sinking feeling that the relative stand-off she had engineered with Mr Anderson would vanish in a second if there was going to be another delay. 'Someone will be here in a few minutes,' Tara whispered, taking over priming the IV fluids. 'It's hell out there.'

Theoretically Leah needed a doctor to start the fluids, she also needed another registered nurse to check the solution she was about to administer, but in her old department she would have barely given it a thought. She would have started the drip and faced the consequences later, knowing she had the back-up of the consultant. Her timing may have been off, but for the first time in more than a year Leah felt a wave of homesickness for her old department, for the team she had so effortlessly run, for the comradeship she had fought so hard to nurture.

But rules were different here, Leah reminded herself, and more to the point she wasn't in charge. The buck didn't stop with Leah—Fay would possibly be in trouble also if Leah went ahead and broke with convention.

'Fill the paediatric burette to two hundred mils,' Leah ordered, 'and set the pump to give a stat bolus dose. By the time you've done that I'll be back.'

Running across the department, she slid open the resus doors. The sight that greeted her not a particularly pretty one and she could see in a glance the reason no one had responded to Tara's pleas for a doctor. Every bed was full, a three-, maybe four-year-old was fitting as the paediatricians fought desperately to stop the convulsions that racked his body, a young man was having his fractured leg reduced, his screams filling the room as the trauma team performed cardiac massage on the end bed.

'I need a doctor in Paed Resus.' Leah spoke above the noise, her eyes meeting Cole's as he looked up briefly. 'Now!' she said firmly, 'or we're going to have a paediatric arrest on top of everything else.'

'I've got this, Cole, you go,' one of the orthopods said, taking the unfortunate young man's leg and carrying on with the reduction as Cole hurried out after Leah.

She relayed the story as best she could as they raced through the department. 'Have you started a drip?'

'I can't do that without a doctor's order,' Leah said,

not missing the quizzical look Cole shot at her as they entered the room.

He nodded as soon as he was at the bedside and Tara passed the bung which Leah connected as Cole examined the infant.

'Has she had any wet nappies today?'

'I don't know,' Mr Anderson answered, clearly agitated as Cole listened to her chest. 'She's had lots of dirty ones, but I don't know if she's been wet.'

'Blood pressure?' Cole asked, his voice clipped, and even though he looked calm Leah could see the lines of tension around his mouth.

'Sixty on thirty.'

'Elevate the foot of the bed and get an NG tube into her while she's still flat. Did you take any blood when you put the IV in?'

'I got enough to do some U and Es and an FBC.'

Handing him the blood forms, Cole scrawled his orders and signature and Leah handed the blood tubes and forms to Tara.

'Get a porter to rush these up and ring the lab and tell them to get straight onto them.'

Cole was examining the little girl gently, pushing her chin down to her chest to check for any neck stiffness, which could be a sign of meningitis, and then carefully examining her ears and throat. As he gently probed her mouth with the lolly stick, Jessica grimaced, feebly trying to push Cole's hand away, which was a good sign indeed as only a few short minutes ago she had barely flinched as Leah had twice stuck needles into her. Looking up, Cole gave Mr Anderson a steadying smile. 'The fluids we're giving her are already starting to have an effect. Hopefully now she'll pick up quickly. I'm still with another patient but I'll write up some IV orders for Jessica and I'll be back very shortly and do a more thorough examination. I know you would have gone through this last night but I'm going to need to get a history from you again.'

Mr Anderson nodded, positively docile now. 'Look, I'm sorry about before.' He gave an embarrassed cough as Cole, who clearly had no idea what had gone on, gave a bemused frown. 'I had a bit of a go at the nurses when I got here. It's just we seemed to be waiting for so long and I was so worried.'

For an instant Leah could have sworn Cole's grip tightened on the pen he was holding, could have sworn his eyes narrowed slightly as he looked up, but even as she registered the fact, Cole righted himself, giving Mr Anderson a brief nod.

'Don't worry about it for now. We're used to agitated patients here.'

Leah had heard it all before, had probably said the exact thing herself on numerous occasions, but today, with her heart rate still topping a hundred, with Mr Anderson's angry shouts still ringing in her ears, Cole's laid-back words incensed Leah. It was all very well for Cole to graciously accept an apology, all very well for Cole to shrug it off as a non-event when it hadn't even touched him, and she didn't return Cole's smile when he looked over at her.

'I'll be back shortly, then,' Cole said, writing on the IV chart before beating a hasty retreat back to a still steaming resus.

Jessica was picking up now and Mr Anderson swallowed back his tears as he cradled his daughter.

'Later on we can give her some fluids down the tube in her nose,' Leah explained as she checked Jessica's obs again, pleased to see they were picking up. 'For now, though, she's getting everything she needs through the drip.'

'Will she still have the diarrhoea?'

'That has to run its course, I'm afraid. We don't give any medication to stop it, but they took a specimen last night so we should get the results through soon and then we'll know what bug's causing it so we'll be better able to tell you how likely it's going to last.'

'Can she have a drink? If she asks for one, I mean.'

Leah nodded. 'She may well vomit it up, but drinking's good.'

A tiny blush crept over Mr Anderson's face. 'Sister, about before, I really am sorry.'

Leah didn't say anything, just fiddled with the blood-pressure monitor, setting the cycle for fifteen minute obs before writing down her findings.

'I was just blowing off a bit of hot air,' Mr Anderson mumbled. 'I would never have hit you, you know?'

Eighteen months ago she would have shrugged it off, accepted his apology and carried right on, only she couldn't do it any more. Couldn't pretend that it didn't matter, that bully-boy tactics didn't hurt. Taking a deep breath, Leah looked up from the chart on which she was writing. 'No, Mr Anderson,' she said softly, as he shifted uncomfortably in his seat. 'I didn't know.'

It took for ever for the department to settle, but finally order was restored and even though the department was still full with a massive backlog in the waiting room at least things seemed manageable. Glancing up at the clock, Leah gave an internal sigh. There was still another hour of her shift to go and all she really wanted to do was go home to sink into a bath and hopefully quell the knot of tension that seemed to be stuck like a fist in her stomach since the confrontation with Mr Anderson.

'How are you doing?' Cole looked over her shoulder as she wrote up some notes.

'Fine,' Leah sighed, 'or at least I will be in an hour or so.'

'It's been a bit like that today, hasn't it?' Cole agreed. As she made to go he called her back. 'Hey, Leah?' He was tapping his pen on the nurses' station in front of him, clearly not quite comfortable with what he was about to say. 'How come you didn't start the drip?'

Turning, Leah gave a small shrug, but her casual gesture belied the sudden glint of tears in her eyes. 'Like I said, I needed a doctor—'

'Oh, come on, Leah.' Cole shook his head. 'You're a charge nurse, for heaven's sake. The kid had been in the night before with gastro and don't hide behind the fact you're a *just* a nurse. You know damn well with your qualifications you would have shut down any argument from Admin in a second. You're paid to make decisions in an emergency. Are you trying to tell me that in England—?'

'But we're not in England.' Her words came out harsh—too harsh, Leah realised, but tears were threatening now. Cole was right. Theoretically he was wrong, but in practice he was right. Any emergency nurse worth her salt would have started that drip and her hesitation truly scared her. 'And I'm not a charge nurse here, Cole, I'm an RN and a bank nurse to boot. If you don't like the rules, if you want nurses starting drips without a doctor's say-so, then you, better than anyone, are in a position to change things. I was just doing my job.'

It was a cop-out and they both knew it, and Cole gave a tight shrug as Leah made to go. Again she didn't get very far, only this time Cole calling her back had nothing to do with it. This time it was Leah making waves.

'In England,' she added, with a defiant note to her voice, 'a grad nurse wouldn't have to beg twice for a doctor to come to the cots.'

'Tara didn't say it was an emergency.'

'Oh, so do you think I sent her in to ask you to come and strap an ankle? And while we're on the subject, in England, or at least in the department I used to work in,' Leah added, with a slight tremble to her voice but not bothering to lower it as Fay came over and shot them both a questioning look, 'if a patient was abusive to a member of staff, the doctor wouldn't just dismiss it out of hand.'

She should have stayed, should have seen it through, but the emergency corridor was hardly the best of locations and, biting on her lip to hold back her tears, Leah made her way to the coffee-room, half expecting Cole to follow her. But it was Fay instead who came in and busied herself pouring a coffee without saying a word.

'I'm sorry, Fay,' Leah said as Fay handed her a steaming cup, 'but despite what you're thinking, that had absolutely nothing to do with the fact Cole and I are seeing each other.'

'I know that,' Fay said shrewdly, 'or this conversation would have been taking place in my office. Mr Anderson really upset you, didn't he?'

Leah gave a small reluctant nod, running a trembling hand through her hair. 'I just got a bit of fright,' Leah said finally. 'And Cole's dismissal infuriated me, though in fairness Cole wasn't there when it all happened. By the time the emergency was over Mr Anderson was as docile as a teddy bear. Cole probably thought he'd just snapped a bit, when in actual fact he was extremely threatening to both Tara and myself.'

'He was probably scared,' Fay said wisely. 'And as for Cole...' Kind, knowing eyes met Leah's. 'I made no secret of my reservations about you two working together, not only to you, Leah, to Cole as well. Happily I've been proved wrong, but the simple fact of the matter is, impartiality might come at a high price sometimes.' Registering Leah's frown, Fay pushed on gently. 'Sometimes when you're trying not to show favouritism you can go too far the other way, and if he came across as impassive it was probably to mask what he was really feeling.'

Leah nodded, remembering Cole's expression when Mr Anderson had attempted to excuse his actions.

'You can't have it both ways, Leah,' Fay said a touch more firmly. 'You can't expect Cole to treat you as a colleague one minute and a defensive lover the next.'

'I know,' Leah admitted, grateful for Fay's insight and embarrassed at the same time. 'I'm more cross with myself really than Cole. That little girl needed a drip, was on the verge of collapse. Normally I would have…' Her voice trailed off as Leah squeezed her eyelids closed on a fresh crop of tears.

'In your other life?' Fay said.

Leah nodded, wiping a stray tear angrily with the back of her hand, determined not to break down completely.

'It must be hard,' Fay said gently. 'Was it busy where you worked?'

Leah nodded, surprisingly grateful for the chance to talk about her old job. 'Pretty much like this. I did nights,' she added, and Fay gave a knowing nod.

'Which means fewer doctors and more pressure?'

'I loved it,' Leah admitted. 'And Cole's right in what he said. I wouldn't have thought twice about starting that drip back home.'

'You would have thought twice,' Fay said perceptively. 'Three times even. You'd have examined the child, known it was gravely ill, and when you'd realised the doctors were stuck, and that no help was forthcoming, you'd have acted. That's what we do each day, Leah, that's what being an emergency nurse is all about—dealing with emergencies. And despite what Cole might say, despite your qualifications, I'm glad that you did hesitate today. I don't want an RN, no matter how well qualified she thinks she is, saying to hell with protocol.'

'I know that,' Leah agreed. 'Even when I was thinking about starting it, I knew that if I did, if things went wrong then it wouldn't just land on my shoulders but yours as well. But I still feel guilty…'

'Because you're over-qualified,' Fay suggested. 'Over-qualified to be just a number. Would it help if I told you there's a clinical nurse specialist position coming up? I know it's not up to the level you were but at least it's a step in the right direction, and if you were on the permanent staff things could surely only be easier?'

Leah looked up sharply, a tremulous smile wobbling on the edge of her lips. 'I thought I was about to get a dressing-down, not offered a promotion.'

'I'm not handing it to you on a plate,' Fay said sternly, but her eyes were kind. 'But I guess, with me as a recent reference, they'd be pretty stupid to say no. It's on nights. I know that's not ideal for a young woman,' Fay added, misinterpreting the frown that flickered on Leah's face, 'but at least you'd have a shoe in, and the way the roster is at the moment there's no doubt that we'd soon be needing you back on days.'

'I'm only on a holiday visa,' Leah said, doubts flowing into her mind with a horrible dousing effect.

Nights!

Nowhere was really safe in Emergency, Mr

Anderson had proved that. Tempers could flare at any given moment, but the thought of permanent nights had Leah in a spin. 'I'm only here until I'm well enough to fly home.'

'Are you, though?' Fay said, standing up as her pager sprang into life. 'This could be home too, Leah. It's up to you.'

'About before,' Leah started as she walked in the door. They hadn't seen each other since her dummy spit in the corridor and, bracing herself for a confrontation, Leah headed up the hall.

'Work's work.' Leaning up against the living-room door, never had Cole looked more divine and never had she loved him more as he came over and kissed her deeply, dismissing her worries in an instant. 'If we're going to work together, we're going to row, but we have to leave it where it belongs—at work,' Cole said softly. 'This is home, we leave the arguments at the door.' He gave a low laugh as Leah pulled her scrunchy out and ran a troubled hand through her hair. 'Mind you, had you came home an hour ago it might have been a different story. I was still smarting.' His eyes narrowed thoughtfully, staring at her for an age before he carried on talking. 'Knowing what you've been through, knowing how hard it is for you, when that guy—'

'I understand, Cole.' Taking a deep breath, Leah carried on talking. 'And what I said before was unfair. The last thing I really wanted was you jumping to my defence. I just didn't realise it at the time.'

'I spoke to him later.' As Leah's eyes widened

Cole gave her a slow, measured smile. 'Don't worry, I was so restrained you'd have been proud of me, but I'm pretty sure the nurses on the children's ward don't have anything to worry about.' He took her hands, staring at them for ever before he carried on. 'I'm a doctor there, Leah. I can't let emotion get in the way and if I'd gone with my initial reaction, if I'd told him what I really thought, well, suffice to say I don't think you'd have been particularly pleased.'

'I wouldn't have,' Leah admitted. 'And I understand that at work you're a doctor and I'm just another nurse, it's just…'

He heard the hesitant note in her voice and his hands gripped hers tighter. 'Say what's on your mind, Leah. It's just what?'

Looking up, she took a deep breath. 'I don't want to be just another nurse.' When Cole didn't respond Leah carried on talking. 'Which seems so strange when until a few weeks ago I didn't even know if I wanted to work in Emergency any more…'

'Until I forced you.'

Leah shrugged. 'Even though it didn't feel like it at the time, I'm actually glad I was pushed into going back. A year running away from things, trying to *find* myself, didn't help a single iota. Jumping back in at the deep end has been the best cure of all. I've loved my time at Melbourne Central, loved not being in charge, finding my feet again without all the pressure. Or at least I did for a while.'

'But not now?'

Leah shook her head. 'I want to be back in charge, Cole. You were right. In England I would have started that drip, and it's made me realise how much I miss my old job. I want to be making the decisions I used to make without even blinking. I want my career back, Cole.'

'Are you saying that you want to go home?' His voice was so low, so quiet Leah had to strain to catch it.

'I don't know.' Gulping she looked up at him. 'Fay offered me a job today. Apparently there's a clinical nurse specialist position coming up...'

'That's fantastic,' Cole started, but when her eyes didn't meet his he changed tack. 'Isn't it?'

'It's not what I was.' Leah shrugged. 'But it's a step in the right direction, I guess, and Fay said once I'd got my foot in the door... But it's on nights, Cole.' The fear in her voice was audible even to Leah. 'I don't know if I can do it.'

'You can do it.' His response was immediate, heartfelt and convincing—everything she hadn't expected. She'd been sure he'd hold her back, sure he'd cast doubts, but instead he was encouraging her. But Leah wasn't sure it was what she wanted to hear.

'Look at how upset I was today...'

'And look at how well you coped. Oh, Leah...' Walking her over to the sofa, he pulled her down beside him, wrapping her in his arms and warming her with his strength. 'I know how you feel...' When she gave him a slightly disbelieving look he pulled her closer. 'I do, Leah. Part of me wants to scream no, to tell you to work on the wards or specialise in docile geriatrics, to do everything I can to keep you safe while the other part...' He gave her a slow smile. 'It's not what you really want, though, is it? It might do for a while, but sooner or later you'd regret it. You have to face your fears, Leah, not keep running from them. You have to deal with the past so you can get on with the future.'

'I thought you'd try to stop me,' Leah admitted. 'I thought you'd tell me it was too soon, too danger-ous…'

'I nearly did.' His honesty stilled her. 'Leah, I've never really thought about the danger in Emergency. Sure, I've been to all the meetings, read the memos Admin hand out, but I've always figured I'd be OK. There're security guards on hand, a direct line to the police station and at the end of the day, as opposed to most of the patients I'm six foot three and sober. But you're not, are you, Leah?'

'I never drink before work.'

Her attempt at humour didn't even raise a smile.

'I don't want you working nights, Leah, I want you home safe with me. That's the truth of the matter but at the end of the day we both know that's not the answer.'

A watery smile hovered on her lips. 'Since when did you get so smart?'

'About eight weeks ago.' His smile matched hers. 'How about I fix dinner?'

'You mean ring for a take-away?'

'At least there won't be any washing-up.' He made to go, but she pulled him back.

'We're all right?' Leah asked. 'I mean, the row at work…'

'Row?' Cole shot her an incredulous look. 'You

call that a row? When Heather was...' Even before his voice faded out Leah knew he'd finished talking, knew from the sudden tension, the set of his jaw that the conversation was over...

That she'd lost him.

'Do you fancy curry?'

Watching him pull the menu off the fridge, watching as he dialled the number and nattered away in familiar tones to the guy on the other end of the phone, Leah felt her heart breaking. Only the pain she was experiencing had nothing to do with work, nothing to do with an angry patient or night duty or a family on the other side of the world, but everything to do with the man who held her in the palm of his hand.

She hadn't lost him, Leah realised.

She'd never really had him in the first place.

CHAPTER NINE

'I KNOW we never get our lunch-breaks together.'
Tara blushed as she helped Leah tuck in a sheet on a
gurney. 'But I asked Fay if someone could cover for
us. I thought it might be nice to have lunch together,
given that it's my last day and everything.'

They were setting up the emergency bay, preparing
for the influx of patients that would invariably start
trickling in any time now. They waved as the night
staff wearily trod past, yawning as they bade their
goodbyes.

For Leah it was the best time of the day. Fresh,
perfumed, her mascara still intact, there was something nice about setting up for a day's work, taking
advantage of the early morning lull, a chance for a
quick gossip and a catch-up before you barely had a
chance to breathe.

'My treat,' Tara added, blushing ever deeper.

'Don't be daft.' Leah grinned. 'If anything, I should
be buying you lunch. You've been a pleasure to work
with.'

'Honestly?'

'Honestly. I can't believe it's eight weeks already
but on the other hand I feel as if we've been working
together for ever. You're a great nurse,' Leah said,
pausing for a moment and meeting Tara's eyes. 'Anyone would want you on their team, and I've told Fay

the same. It's been great working with you, Tara, but as for lunch…' Leah gave an apologetic smile. 'I'm afraid we're going to have to take a rain check—I've got an appointment with Mr Crean scheduled in my lunch-break.'

'To find out your results?'

Leah nodded. 'He's going to tell me whether or not I'm fit to fly.'

'You've had all your tests then?'

Leah nodded.

'And do you think you've passed?'

When Leah didn't answer straight away Tara carried on relentlessly, rolling her eyes in the general direction of Cole who marched past with barely a greeting, damp hair curling on his collar, holding a steaming mug of coffee, wafting aftershave and managing to look moody and gorgeous and sexy all at once. Leah felt her insides turn to liquid. Oh, he could feign nonchalance, he could beg indifference, but Leah had been there that morning, had massaged the shampoo into that hair, watched as he'd splashed on the aftershave, and the reason Cole desperately needed a coffee in his hand was because quite simply this morning there hadn't been time.

'Or more to the point.' Tara broke into Leah's thoughts with pinpoint accuracy. 'Do you want to have passed?'

Leah's eyes met Tara's. For someone who'd just celebrated their twenty-second birthday Tara was way too clued in!

'OK, scrub lunch.' Leah grinned. 'How about a

long dinner and a few too many glasses of wine? I could use some insight.'

'Done.'

Leah was never quite sure how it happened after that, whether Fay called her over or Leah merely looked up as the trimphone went off. The trimphone was a direct line to Ambulance Control and normally it meant that the paramedics were bringing someone particularly unwell in or that an emergency team needed to be despatched. Seeing Fay pick it up, Leah relaxed, knowing the call was being dealt with, but somewhere between shaking Tara's hand over the gurney and giving some sort of adolescent high five Fay's eyes locked with hers and the urgency in them had Leah's heart sinking like a stone.

'We should go to that Thai restaurant...' Tara's voice as it was then was the last fleeting sign of normality, the last sound of innocence before chaos took over.

'"Train crash".' As she joined Fay by the trimphone Leah read out loud Fay's hastily written notes on the sticky pad as Tara's eyes widened in horror. '"Multiple injuries".' Swallowing hard, Leah read the last few words with a slight tremor in her voice as Fay underlined them, scouring two heavy lines into the paper as suddenly everything changed.

'"Possible major incident"!'

'Is this a set-up?' A nervous grin wobbled on Tara's face. 'Is this one of those mock-ups they tell us about?'

'I'm afraid not.' Fay's voice had a slight edge to it as she came off the phone, but apart from that she looked as calm and as unflappable as ever. 'Dan.' Fay addressed the hovering security guard. 'Go and round up any night emergency staff still in the car park.' Turning to the gathering staff members, mainly addressing Cole, she passed on what she had heard. 'There's been a train crash on the Gembrook line. Unfortunately it would seem that it's two commuter trains. They want us to send out a team.'

'Is that all we've got?' Cole asked. 'Have we any idea of the numbers, how fast they were going?'

'Not at this stage. Apparently access is difficult. It's in the hills and the crash has taken place down an embankment. No one has been able to get down to the injured yet and make a formal assessment. All the major hospitals in the area are being put on standby and asked to send teams. It has the potential for the numbers to be huge, but until they get access…'

'Start the disaster plan,' Cole broke in. 'Get everyone in. It's the rush hour so we could be talking in the hundreds here. Anyway, if I've called it too soon, we're due for a practice.'

'This isn't a practice, then?' Tara asked again, her lips white, still hoping for a nudge and a grin that this wasn't a real unfolding tragedy as Fay picked up one of many ringing phones.

'The chopper is ready, Cole.'

'Let's get onto it, then.' Cole was heading towards the ambulance bay, pulling off his tie and shirt as he did so. 'Who are the nurses down to go out on the squad today?'

'Louise and Vicki,' Fay ordered, following the staff out. At any given time the disaster plan was ready to implement. Each shift two nurses were allocated to go on any callouts, but no one had been expecting this!

Leah helped Vicki into her overalls, finding her a hard hat as she hauled on an emergency backpack.

'Maybe you should go,' Vicki said through chattering teeth. 'You're way more qualified than I am.'

'No.' Cole broke in quickly, too quickly. 'You're not on the trauma team,' he offered by way of explanation, but it was woefully inadequate and Leah shot him a look, warning him he was crossing the line. Yes, it might be dangerous, yes, it would be bloody and, of course, his first instinct was to protect her but, as Cole had pointed out, work and home were two different things.

He wasn't her lover here.

'You'll be fine, Vicki,' Leah said firmly, her eyes meeting Cole's briefly. His face was expressionless, a muscle flickering in his cheek the only indication of his tension. 'You'll be fine,' Leah said again, only this time it was to Cole.

'Take care,' she added in a whisper, which wasn't much of a goodbye but it was all there was time for.

Even though she was in a different country to her own, Leah knew exactly what to do. The department snapped into disaster mode, ward staff coming down to collect their patients, the walking wounded in the waiting room advised to come back later or to go and visit their local GP. Areas were set up in colour codes so that as the patients from the accident started to come in they could be triaged and sent to the appropriate area. Leah had done it before—there had been a crash on the underground, a stampede at a rock concert and she'd run the show—but as the department quietened, as an uneasy silence filled the waiting rooms, as the staff crowded around the television, a growing sense of unease started to fill Leah, a sense that today was going to be the worst yet.

'Shouldn't the patients be starting to arrive now?' Tara asked, her initial surge of adrenaline starting to wear off.

'I would have thought so,' Leah said thoughtfully, staring at the television screen and trying to comprehend that the images she was seeing were real. 'But, look, there's no access, the ambulances can't get down there.'

'Leah, can I have a word?' Fay came off the phone and gestured her to one side. 'This is bad.' For the first time Leah heard a hint of nervousness in her boss's voice. 'I've just heard from Ambulance Control that the casualty figures are huge, but they can't get the injured up. They're setting up an emergency area at the scene, but it could be a while before casualties start to arrive.'

'And we'll be ready,' Leah said assuredly. 'It's good Cole didn't hang around before calling a major incident.'

'They want us to send another team.' Her eyes never left Leah's face. 'They need the best out there, Leah, and I know you're on the roster as an RN, but you've been out to stuff like this before. Do you mind going?'

Immediately Leah nodded, Cole's warning flying out of her mind. Fay was her boss, Fay was the one calling the shots, and Leah was not only able but willing. 'Sure.'

'I've spoken to the nurse supervisor and I'll sort it out with the pay office,' Fay said, following Leah out to the storeroom.

'Don't be daft.' Leah shrugged. It seemed ridiculous to be talking about money at a time like this but as Fay pulled down some overalls and hesitated for a fraction of a second before handing them over, Leah realised she'd missed the point.

'I'm not being daft. You're going to be making decisions out there, big ones, and you'll have the department's back-up.'

Only then did it register she was actually going, that the images she had seen on the television she would be witnessing at first hand, and the enormity of the task ahead started to sink in. 'Thanks, Fay.'

She'd never been in a helicopter, but there wasn't exactly time to appreciate the view. Jenny, a nurse from nights Leah had only said good morning or good evening to, gave her a wan smile as over and over they checked the supplies in the emergency backpack they'd been issued with, along with the leather pouch containing drugs that hung around her waist, knowing they'd need to put their hand on things in an instant. Samuel Donovan, whom Leah had first met when she'd been admitted and had worked alongside since, pulled up drugs and taped the ampoules to the syringes and gave Leah a reassuring nod as their eyes met for a moment. Leah took a cleansing breath, knowing she was part of a good team, but as they neared the scene and Leah got her first glimpse of the disaster site, nerves started to catch up with her.

She'd been told two trains had been involved, but the gnarled stretch of metal blended into one, the front or back carriages, Leah couldn't be sure which, were precariously on their sides, rising in an ugly peak. She saw the fluoroscent jackets of the firefighters as they walked along the top of the wreckage, the red crosses on the vests of the emergency personnel and a massive white tent set up alongside, before the scene disappeared from view and the helicopter descended to the ground.

'Keep your head down,' Samuel shouted, as they jumped out and ran the distance to the circus of flashing lights. Ambulances, fire engines and police cars were everywhere, their lights blazing like those at a fairground, but the surreal sight of empty ambulances reminded Leah of the emergency department, how horrible it was that people who so desperately needed it were trapped beyond help's reach. A swift handover was delivered as they peered over the embankment edge, the sound of the jaws of life shearing through the carriage roofs jarring every tooth in Leah's jaw.

'Ever done abseiling?' Jenny asked through chattering teeth as they climbed into leather hoists, and Leah gave a nervous laugh.

'Once. And I swore never again.'

Thank heavens there hadn't been time for breakfast, Leah thought as they slowly walked their way down the side of the embankment. It wasn't abseiling exactly but it came precariously close, and every time the rope slackened Leah's stomach took a dive. She only remembered to breathe again when two firefighters reached up and pulled her the last couple of feet to solid ground.

It looked like a war scene, or at least what Leah imagined a war scene would look like. Bloodied, shocked victims were walking along the track, there were bodies sprawled by the trackside, some beyond help, others moaning piteously. 'Over here, Doctor.' A paramedic was frantically signalling to Samuel and he turned to Leah and Jenny.

'I'll follow you in as soon as I can.'

'Carriage four,' a burly man shouted. 'We've sprayed the number on the outside, we've just got access. You three can take that one. We got some of the walking wounded out through the window.'

They would have run, but the terrain prevented them, the inaccessibility of the area being rammed home deeper every minute. The ear-splitting sound of glass being broken in the next carriage filled the air as Leah was hauled by the firefighter to the carriage roof where she balanced on the sloping edge, clinging on as the carriage gave a lurch.

'We're doing our best to secure it,' the firefighter roared above the noise of the cutting equipment and breaking glass. 'More stuff should be arriving soon.'

Only then did the danger of the situation she had placed herself in really hit home but, hearing the moans of the trapped victims inside, nerves and fear left Leah. Her only thought was to get in, to help, but they couldn't just yet. The newly created exit offered a means of escape to some of the better-off victims and the next frustrating fifteen minutes were spent hauling them out one by one and lowering them into the welcoming arms of the paramedics before they could finally be lowered in themselves.

How?

The word resounded in her head like a mantra as her eyes slowly focused on the scene.

How were they supposed to free these people?

How could they possibly work in this bloodied, gnarled mess?

How could they possibly choose who they helped first?

'Daddy.' A tiny whimper reached her and Leah's eyes fixed on the terrified face of a little girl. She crawled over, a massive jolt of the carriage startling her, again ramming home the precariousness of her own situation. Her hand lurched forward to the twisted seat the girl was somehow still sitting in, but up close Leah could see why—the seats in front were flattened like an accordion, pinning the child and her father together.

'Daddy,' she moaned again, and Leah looked over, bracing herself for the worst but giving a relieved, steadying smile as she saw he was conscious.

'Its OK, Stacey, Daddy's here.' His eyes met Leah's. 'Get her out, will you?' he begged, and Leah gave a small nod.

'As soon as we can.' In a matter of seconds Leah assessed the small child, attaching a cervical collar first, her fingers working their way down and realising with sweet relief that she seemed relatively unharmed.

'How are you, sir?' Leah asked.

'Don't worry about me—just get her out.'

'We will,' Leah said assuredly, feeling for his pulse as she spoke. 'My name's Leah. I'm a nurse.'

'Greg.'

'Greg, we're going to get you both out just as soon as we can.' Her voice was calm but Greg's inactivity was unnerving Leah. He was talking to his daughter, trying to reassure her, but he remained still, not looking over, just staring fixedly ahead as Leah tried to climb towards him. 'Are you hurt anywhere?'

There was the longest pause. Shining her torch into his face, Leah inched her way over. 'Greg, where are you hurt?'

'I can't feel my legs.'

Shining her torch down, she prayed for a twist of metal, something that might be pinning them, but with a nervous gulp she looked at the relatively clear space around them, at the absence of any clear injury, and her heart sank.

'Just get Stacey out.'

'I need you to stay still, Greg,' Leah said, her tone firm, praying the carriage wouldn't jolt again as she unclipped a hard cervical collar from her bag.

'I've broken my neck, haven't I?'

Leah knew she should be honest, knew that the truth was needed, but until that hard collar was in place she didn't want Greg getting any more upset. The chances were he *had* broken his neck but, with luck, could be an incomplete fracture or swelling causing the paraplegia. The slightest movement could worsen his injury and render the damage irreversible so it was imperative he stay still.

'Greg,' Leah said again, moving ever closer and

trying not to create any movement of the seats herself, 'you have to stay still. I'm going to put a collar on you and then we can talk, but until we do I don't want you to move. Now, don't talk, don't nod, don't do anything—just let me do all the work.

'Samuel!' Leah called into the darkness, not sure if he was in the carriage yet but knowing she was going to need him. 'I need a hand over here.'

'What have you got?' The voice that greeted her was as unexpected as it was familiar, and Leah started slightly as she heard Cole's voice. She didn't doubt he knew she was in there, didn't doubt he wasn't particularly pleased at the fact, but there was no time to worry about it now. Lives were at stake.

She knew Cole needed an answer, knew he had to weigh up Leah's demands with whatever he was dealing with, but, not wanting to upset Greg with his neck still unstable, she didn't want to shout out that Greg had a spinal injury, worried the effect the words would have on her patient. 'I need a hand to get a neck collar on,' Leah called, hoping that despite her rather vague reply Cole would read between the lines and realise the urgency behind her summons.

He must have, because in a few minutes he was beside her, taking in the situation in an instant. 'I'm just going to climb over you.' He smiled down at the little girl. 'What's your name?'

'Stacey,' Leah answered for her when it was clear she wasn't going to. 'And this is Greg, her dad.'

'OK, Stacey, my name's Cole, I'm a doctor. I'm going to climb over you and I'll try not to knock you, but I need to get to your dad so I want you to stay as still as you can for me.' He spoke as he moved, all the time reassuring the terrified little girl as he inched his way over. 'That's the chap,' Cole said gently, holding Greg's head firmly in place as Leah struggled to fit the collar in the horribly confined space. 'Get a line into him,' Cole ordered, when finally the cervical collar was firmly in place. 'He could go into shock. Run through some Gelofusion and, even though the collar's still in place, warn him that it's imperative he still stays absolutely still.'

'Will do.' Leah nodded as Cole called out his instructions and for a moment so small it was barely there the tension seemed to fade from his face, a flicker of a reassuring smile winging his way to Leah as he comforted her with his eyes.

'Samuel's trackside, working on someone, so if you need a doctor call out for me. But I need to get back to my patient now. I'll tell the paramedics we need a spinal board to move Greg. Hopefully we can clear some space and let more help in.'

'Go,' Leah said, then changed her mind. 'Cole, can you get Stacey out?'

Leah knew the little girl wasn't a medical priority, but this was surely no place for her to be. 'There are no obvious injuries, apart from cuts and bruises,' Leah added as Cole made a swift assessment and gave a quick nod.

'Stacey?' Despite his urge to get back to his patient, despite the direness of the situation, Cole took his time to speak slowly to the little girl, knowing if he upset her now there was no way she would comply. 'We're going to get you out. You see that light

over there? That's where the firemen have cut a hole
so you can escape, that's what all that horrible noise
was. Now, it isn't far, but you're going to have to
help me by being brave. I need you to climb up onto
my shoulders and hold around my neck.'

'Like a piggy-back,' Leah said. 'You can do that,
can't you?'

As the little girl gave a wide-eyed nod of agree-
ment Leah let out a relieved sigh, gently prising her
out of her seat as Cole struggled to remain patient.
But suddenly Stacey changed her mind, pitiful frightened sobs escaping her lips as she called for her father, refusing to leave his side.

'Stacey.' Cole's voice was a touch louder but still
gentle. 'Daddy needs a special sort of stretcher. Now,
you're going to have to help me get one for him.
We're going to crawl to the light and when the firemen lift you out I want you to say in a very loud
voice that they need to help your daddy and fetch him
a stretcher. Do you think you can do that?'

It was probably a matter of seconds but it felt like
minutes before finally Stacey calmed down, nodding
bravely as Leah lifted her over and placed her on
Cole's shoulders.

'She's OK now,' Leah said. Turning back to Greg,
she wrapped a tourniquet round his arm and ran
through a flask. They even managed to share a wry
smile as she found a passenger strap exactly where it
should be, the ideal place to hang the fluids. 'Cole's
taking her out to safety, so let's see about you.'

'I'm paralysed, aren't I?' Now his daughter was
safely taken care of, Greg could concentrate on him-

self and voice his fears. 'I've broken my neck, haven't I?'

'We don't know that yet,' Leah said gently. 'Until we get you to hospital we won't know exactly what's going on. There could be any number of things causing your weakness but, as the doctor said, it really is imperative that you stay still.'

'Don't lie to me.' Greg was sobbing now and Leah felt a surge of panic. The collar was secure but if Greg started thrashing around untold damage could be done. If his fracture extended, he could even stop breathing.

'You mustn't move,' Leah warned as Greg attempted to lurch forward, hysteria overwhelming him. 'If you move you could die,' Leah said sharply, knowing it was all or nothing but praying that her words would still him.

'I'd rather die,' Greg sobbed. 'I'd rather be dead than spend the rest of my life in a wheelchair.'

Glancing over, she watched as Cole mercifully reached the exit, watched as strong hands reached in and lifted Stacey to safety. As much as Greg mightn't think it now, he still had a lot to be thankful for.

'No, Greg,' Leah said firmly, her eyes locking on her patient's. Something in her voice stilled him, something in her voice told Greg that now wasn't the time for dramatics. 'No, Greg,' Leah repeated, 'you wouldn't.'

CHAPTER TEN

'THEY'RE calling us out.'

Leah could hear Cole coming towards her but she didn't look up. She was too busy concentrating on her patient, too busy counting the compressions in her head as she administered cardiac massage to a woman younger than herself. Greg had been safely lifted out, but that hadn't been the end of it. Stacey and Greg had been the tip of the iceberg, Greg's safe evacuation paving the torturous way to yet more grief.

Only the woman's head and chest were exposed and at first Leah had been sure she was dead and had braced herself to move on to the next victim, to look after the living, help someone who had a chance, but a faint flicker of a pulse at the woman's neck had been enough for Leah to do her best for this stranger.

To afford her a chance.

'One of the carriages has caught fire, Leah,' Cole shouted as she carried on with the cardiac massage. 'They want all emergency personnel out till it's clear.'

'She had a pulse when I got to her.' Leah looked up at him frantically as Cole shone a light in the woman's eyes.

'Stop the massage.' Putting his stethoscope in his ears, Cole slipped the bulb over the woman's chest, screwing up his face in concentration as he listened for a heartbeat, a breath sound, any indication that she was still alive.

Leah didn't take the chance of a tiny reprieve. Instead, she concentrated on pulling at the seat that was pinning the woman to the floor, tugging at it with all her might but still not able to move it.

'She's dead,' Cole said gently, his eyes locking on Leah's. 'There's nothing we can do, Leah. We have to get out.'

'The electricity's off,' Leah said, trying helplessly to free her patient. 'It's not a diesel train, the whole thing isn't about to go up. We'll be all right.'

But Cole shook his head. 'They think someone used a lighter to see, and a whole carriage has gone up. They're dousing the carriage with foam and with the extra weight any minute now this whole lot could topple.'

She was about to agree, to give a reluctant nod, but the seat she had been pulling suddenly gave way. Too little, too late, Leah thought with a sob of frustration, as she toppled backwards. As she righted herself, as she started to crawl for the exit, she stopped in her tracks, frowning in bemusement as Cole recommenced the cardiac massage.

'Did you get a pulse?' Ignoring the shouts to get out from the firefighters, Leah inched her way back over, but as her head torch shone on the now exposed body of her patient Leah felt her heart somewhere in her mouth as the soft mound of her patient's stomach caught in her torchlight.

'She's pregnant,' Leah gasped, watching as Cole pulled out an ambu-bag and placed it over the woman's mouth, pushing air into her lungs as Leah instinctively took over the massage.

'She had a pulse when you got to her?' Cole's eyes met hers and though Leah was sure, as positive as she could be, for a second or two she wavered, knowing the implications of her answer. If the answer was yes, if there was a chance her body had been adequately oxygenated until Leah had arrived, then an emergency Caesarean section would have to be considered.

'A faint one,' Leah said, her voice wavering, bile rising in her throat at the preposterousness of the decision they were nearing.

'Keep up the massage,' Cole ordered, his hands moving down to the woman's groin, feeling for her femoral artery. 'She's got a good output with the massage.' She could see the sweat pouring down his dirtied face, the indecision in his eyes, the tension grooved on every feature as he again reinflated the patient's lungs with the ambu-bag. The fact that the woman had a good femoral pulse meant that the baby could still be getting oxygen, could still be alive, and Leah's eyes shuttered closed for a second as she rhythmically pounded the woman's chest, keeping out the world that was forcing this most awful decision upon them.

'She's dead, Leah.' Cole's eyes were there when hers opened, 'We both know that there's nothing we can do for this lady, she's definitely gone, but there is a chance we could save her baby.'

Leah nodded, words failing her.

'Leah?' She heard the question in his voice, but

knew deep down that the choice had already been made for them.

It was made every day when they clipped on their name badges and headed for work, it was made every time they rolled up for their shift and went in to bat to save strangers' lives. And just because they weren't in the relatively safe confines of a resuscitation room with a full team to support them, just because no one on earth would blame them for walking away now, Leah knew what needed to be done.

All life was precious, all life was valuable, and no matter what the circumstances this baby deserved a chance.

'What do you want me to do?' She couldn't look at him, couldn't bear to see her indecision reflected in his eyes.

'Bag her for me,' Cole said, his voice wavering slightly as he pulled open his backpack and set up his equipment. 'And keep up the massage till I tell you to stop, then I'll need you to shine the torch for me.'

It was soon over.

But it was the longest few minutes of her life.

Even under the controlled setting of Theatre, emergency Caesarean sections were amazingly quick, but here, more than ever, time was of the essence, and as Cole ordered her to stop the massage an involuntary sob escaped Leah's lips. She held the torch with one hand and tried to assist with the other, her breath strangling her as Cole deftly lifted out the pale, limp infant, professional detachment not getting a look-in, tears coursing down both their cheeks as they concentrated on the baby Cole was holding, vigorously rubbing its back as Leah struggled with a rudimentary portable suction machine, trying to clear the baby's airway, tickling the baby's feet to stimulate its breathing. Grabbing the ambu-bag, she turned the mask upside down. An adult mask was way too big for a baby, but used upside down enough of a seal could be created. Just when she thought it was useless, that this horrible, horrible choice had been in vain, she felt the tiniest resistance, felt a limp limb stiffen as it flexed into life, the delicious sound of a splutter as the baby took it's first independent breath.

'Get out now, Leah!' Cole ordered. 'I'll bring the baby.'

But Leah knew that was easier said than done. The path back was precarious enough without holding a slippery baby. Ignoring his orders, pulling off her bag, Leah grabbed at some sterile drapes. Ripping open the pack, she wrapped a sling around Cole, her hands trembling as she secured the baby to his chest, allowing him to crawl more freely.

'Leah, out.'

She nodded. She knew she had to go, knew they had to get out, but there was one more thing she had to do first. Taking one of the remaining drapes, she gently placed it over her patient.

'Your baby's going to be OK,' Leah whispered, her eyes blurring with tears as she finally headed for the exit herself.

The glare of the midmorning sun hit her as Leah was hauled out of the carriage and lowered to safety. The paramedics relieved Cole of his precious bundle, moving as swiftly as they were able towards the triage tent. And though she ached to follow to see how the baby was doing, she took a moment to get her breath, to somehow assimilate all she had witnessed before facing it again. Squinting upwards, she could see the news cameras homing in for their shots, the wail of sirens, busy now as they ferried patients to hospital. Never had a bottle of water tasted better as she gulped the icy liquid. Sucking the sweet fresh air into her lungs, gazing at the lush green trees, it was hard to believe the carnage she had just witnessed.

'Where's Cole?' Blinking, she looked around as Samuel came over. 'Is he over at Triage?'

'Give him a minute or two, Leah. He's pretty shaken up.'

'Following Samuel's gaze, she saw Cole hunched by a tree, squatting down, his head in his hands, his face grey, and Leah knew how ever hard this morning's events had been for her. For Cole it would have been devastating. Ignoring the suggestion to leave him, she made her way over, offering him the drink bottle for something to do because, quite simply, she didn't know what to say.

'I'd better get back.' Accepting the bottle, he took a long drink before heading back to the train.

'It's not secure yet,' Leah called after him, half running to catch up with his long measured strides, only stopping when Samuel caught up with them.

'We're to head back to the hospital now.' When Cole shook his head, Samuel carried on talking. 'They want fresh teams in the carriages and, as much as I don't like it, Cole, you know that's right. We're needed back at the hospital.' His eyes raked the scene and Leah did the same. Cole continued to stare fixedly ahead.

'Hell, it's a bloody mess, isn't it?' Samuel sighed. 'Was it you two who delivered the baby?'

Leah nodded but didn't elaborate, anxious eyes darting to Cole who still wouldn't look at her.

'He's picking up,' Samuel said, and Leah looked over sharply.

'It was a little boy?'

Samuel nodded. 'You did a great job, it must have been hell.' Worried, knowing eyes drifted to Cole as Samuel carried on talking. 'If you want to fill me in, Cole, when they locate the father I can talk to him for you,' he offered. 'Given what's happened, I know it might be a bit much—'

'I'll be fine,' Cole said grimly, staring fixedly ahead as he walked.

'Still, the father's going to be pretty upset...'

'Why?' Cole shouted, calling over his shoulder as he marched angrily ahead. 'At least he got to keep one of them.'

CHAPTER ELEVEN

STARING dry-eyed at the television screen, Leah barely moved as Cole's key turned in the lock. She'd been home a couple of hours now, and even though the news was blaring, even though she held the remote in her hand, Leah barely noticed the horrific images that flashed into the living room, barely even noticed when her own face appeared grim and dirty as a firefighter hauled her out of a carriage.

It was Cole who saturated her mind now.

Cole the root of her pain.

'Did you hear anything?' Leah asked as Cole came through to the living room, putting down his briefcase then heading for the coffee-machine. 'No one's said anything about the baby on the news yet.'

'The hospital wanted to let the father know first, that's why nothing's been on yet,' Cole said wearily, shooting a baleful eye at the television. 'No doubt any minute now it will be the headlines.'

'You've spoken to him?'

Cole nodded, running a weary hand across his forehead before spending an inordinate amount of time watching his coffee trickle into the cup as Leah stared at him expectantly.

'How was he?'

Cole gave a tight shrug. 'I don't want to talk about it, Leah.'

She watched as he went through the milk and sugar routine, watched as he pulled out a packet of biscuits then changed his mind and tossed them back in the cupboard before picking up his drink and taking a sip.

'Well, I do.' His cup paused midway from his mouth and Leah's heart rate did the same thing as her voice rang around the room. 'I was there today, Cole, I helped you deliver that baby, remember, and I have every right to ask how the father is coping. And I have every right to ask you how you're coping, how you're dealing with today, after what happened to Heather.'

Heather.

She felt as if she'd sworn in front of her parents, ordered a rare steak in a vegetarian restaurant, crossed that line Cole instinctively drew, but there was no going back now.

'Samuel told me to give you some space today, Cole. Told me you were bound to be upset, given how Heather had died and everything.' He was slopping his coffee down the sink now, dragging off his tie as he headed for the stairs. 'I thought he was just talking about the baby!'

Her words reached him, stilling him momentarily, his hand reaching for the banister and gripping it.

'Heather broke her neck. You were jet-skiing and Heather broke her neck, and I had to hear it from a colleague of yours. I had to find out how your wife died from someone I occasionally work with.'

Still he didn't move, still he didn't turn, and Leah was consumed with almost a sense of savagery, an outrage at his refusal to face her.

'What difference does it make?' He sounded genuinely bewildered as he finally turned to face her. 'She's dead, Leah, why do the details matter so much to you?'

'Because they clearly matter to you. Cole, I understand you're hurting, I understand why you might be a bit over-protective at times and sometimes mightn't want to talk, or at least as much as I can understand without you letting me in.

'Samuel told me you were on holiday, ''whooping'' it up, when it happened.' She gave an incredulous laugh but it was utterly devoid of humour. 'I can't even picture it, Cole. I can't imagine you ''whooping'' it up, and yet I know that part of you is there. I know that it's deep inside you, only you won't let me see it. I don't want half a relationship, Cole, I don't want to walk on eggshells, avoiding issues, pretending everything's all right.'

'Everything is all right.' He was heading up the stairs now, the conversation obviously over, calling over his shoulder, and Leah raced after him.

'No, it isn't,' Leah shouted. 'Today was bloody and horrible and terrible and yet you're walking away from me, and if you take another step I'm walking out of that door.' She watched as he froze, watched as he slowly turned to face her. 'I can't do this any more, Cole. I can't pretend everything's going to be all right when it clearly isn't.'

'You're tired,' Cole said firmly, 'tired and exhausted, and now really isn't the time—'

'Now's exactly the right time.' For someone who cried at the drop of a hat, the absence of tears surprised even Leah. Her voice if not steady was amazingly clear as she summoned the strength to utter the hardest words of her life. 'You told me to face things, Cole, you told me to stop running away from my problems, and as hard as it is to say what I'm about to say—you were right.'

She watched his face as she spoke, watched his face mask into a pained, stricken dignity as the truth finally came out. 'I don't want to be a clinical nurse specialist, Cole. I don't want to be half of what I am, but I would have accepted it, I'd take the job in an instant if I thought I had all of you.'

'You do,' Cole started, then stopped as Leah broke in.

'I have the bits you want me to see, the bits you're prepared to share, but I'm sorry, Cole, it's simply not enough. I want all of you and you're simply not prepared to give it.' When he didn't say anything Leah answered her own unspoken question.

'I'm going home, Cole.'

'You don't know if you're well enough yet.'

'I spoke to Dr Crean in Emergency this afternoon.' For a second she was sure his impassive mask slipped, was sure she saw a flash of pain in his eyes, but in an instant he snapped back, those guarded eyes shutting her out as she carried on talking. 'My tests were fine. I can go home any time I want.'

'I think running away would be a more apt description.' His lips curled in almost a sneer. 'Just as you did when the going got tough in England.'

His words hurt, hurt more than she thought she could bear, but Leah stood resolute. 'I'm not running away, Cole, I'm facing up to my problems. I need to go back, I need to confront my fears, and hopefully then I'll get over them.'

'Am I supposed to hear angels?' Sarcasm was dripping off his tongue. 'Am I supposed to give a slow handclap at your amazing analogy and thank you for your insight?'

'No.' Tears were starting now but Leah barely noticed, watching as he carried on up the stairs and slammed the bedroom door. 'I just want you to talk to me.'

Because Leah didn't want things to move particularly quickly, because deep down she still prayed for some sort of resolution, for her rather dramatic gesture to force in Cole a realisation, the world suddenly seemed to go on fast forward. A flight was arranged with one speedy call, and it wasn't as if she had much to organise: just a bank account to close and her backpack to fill which saw her through to ten a.m.

Cole had left for work that morning without a goodbye, the front door slamming as she lay in the single bed she'd never slept in, staring at the lemon walls and wondering if it was memories of the past or just plain old pride that had stopped him coming in to her.

And she'd wanted him to come in, Leah admitted to herself. Wanted him to take her in his arms and give to her the piece of him she so desperately needed, to trust her enough to share. But instead she'd lain alone, staring into the darkness and wondering how something so wonderful could have gone so horribly wrong.

'I'm sorry, Fay,' Leah had said when she'd finally plucked up the courage to ring, the front door's echo still ringing in her ears. 'I know I'm leaving you short today.'

'We'll survive,' Fay had said kindly. 'I don't know what's gone on and I can't be sure if this will help or make things worse, but you know that there's always a job here for you if ever you do change your mind. Are you still there?' Fay had checked when Leah hadn't answered.

'Still here,' Leah had squeaked, trying to keep the sob from her voice. 'I'll drop in my uniforms and name tag this morning.'

'Cole can bring them some other time,' Fay had suggested but Leah had shaken her head into the phone.

'I'd rather not leave things for him. Anyway, I've got to pick up my medical certificate from Dr Crean's secretary. As soon as my things are out of the drier I'll head over.'

It felt strange to be walking into Emergency in her shorts and a T-shirt, still part of the team only not quite belonging. And even though she wasn't sure if she wanted to see him, to prolong the agony further, instinctively her eyes scanned the department, knowing, just knowing in an instant that Cole wasn't around.

'How are you?' Fay said gently. 'I'm not being nosy, I was just wondering how you're coping after yesterday.'

'It's our job.' Leah shrugged but Fay wasn't about to be fobbed off.

'You're even starting to sound like Cole. It was a bit more than just another day at the office yesterday, Leah. There's nothing wrong in talking about it.'

'I know,' Leah admitted. 'It was hell out there.'

'Greg Wells is doing well.' Fay smiled as she watched Leah's reaction. 'It was an incomplete fracture apparently and they stabilised it in Theatre. He's already got some sensation in his lower limbs, so there's one happy ending for you.' Taking the bundle of clothes, Fay gave her a warm smile. 'Perhaps you should keep your name tag for half an hour or so?'

'Why?' Leah asked.

'Isn't there someone you'd like to see before you head off?' As Leah shook her head Fay went on, 'I'm not talking about our mutual boss. There's a little baby up in Special Care, doing very nicely thanks to you. Without a security tag you won't get in, they'll think you're the press or something. I think it would be good for you to go and see him—maybe it will put things into perspective a bit for you. Yesterday's events are going to stay with you for ever and seeing what you achieved might help you look back on it with a bit of comfort.'

Taking the tag back from Fay's hands, Leah gave a small nod. 'Thanks, Fay.'

'What time's your flight?'

'Nine p.m.'

'Do you need a lift to the airport or anything?'

Leah shook her head. 'I'd really rather be on my

own. I'd probably rot your leather upholstery I'll be crying so much.'

'Does Cole know? Your flight time, I mean?'

Leah shook her head. 'I only just found it out my-self.' She looked at Fay's slightly startled expression. 'He knows I'm going, though, he just doesn't know all the flight details.'

'Can I tell him,' Fay suggested. 'If he asks, I mean.'

Leah gave a thin smile as she kissed her colleague on the cheek. 'You can, but he won't ask, Fay. It's over.'

Pushing the bell outside the special care unit, Leah gazed through the windows, watching the babies, the monitors flashing, with eyes so full she could barely see.

'You wanted to see baby Heal.' A nurse came out and greeted her. 'I'm Ann, the unit manager. Fay just rang and said you were on your way up.'

'I did,' Leah said in a choked voice, 'but I've changed my mind. I'll just look from here, thanks.'

'Are you sure?' Ann checked. 'I reckon you de-serve a little cuddle. I've just come back from my coffee, but he was fine when I went. We're keeping him in Special Care for twenty-four hours' observa-tion.' Squinting through the window, she looked over to baby Heal's crib. 'His dad's in there, holding him. I'm sure he'd like to meet you.'

'It isn't his dad,' Leah said softly.

Even though he was dressed in a robe with a cap and mask on and his back to her, she'd have recognised Cole anywhere. 'That's the doctor who delivered him.'

'Cole Richardson?' Ann peered harder. 'It is, too. This must be so hard for him. He lost his own baby and wife not so long ago. I expect the world must seem a pretty cruel place to him right now. Are you sure you don't want to come through?'

Leah nodded, not trusting herself to speak, just staring through the window at Cole cradling the baby gently in his arms, wishing she could go over and help him, wishing she could be there as he took this most difficult step.

Maybe her words had reached him, maybe he was trying to move on, but she simply couldn't take that chance, couldn't risk falling back into his arms only to be shut out again when the horrors of their row receded.

Knowing she was right didn't make things easier, though.

Lingering till the final boarding call, Leah longed for resolution. Even as the silver doors of the customs checkpoint slid open and she passed the point of no return, she scanned the crowd for one final glimpse, knowing if he called her name her resistance would shatter in an instant, unable to believe that he'd let her go without putting up some sort of fight.

Once on the plane, she squeezed into her window seat, politely refusing the attempts at conversation from her fellow travellers, painfully recalling the last time she had been on a plane, still hoping against hope for an impassive announcement from the cabin crew asking if a Miss Leah Jacobs could please make herself known to the crew, for Cole to do something, anything, to prevent her from leaving.

But as the cabin door closed, as the plane taxied along the runway and lifted majestically into the dark Melbourne sky, even Leah admitted defeat.

Sinking back into her seat, she huddled into her blanket, didn't even attempt the meal or watch the movie, didn't even shed a tear.

Just stared out at the navy emptiness and tried to get used to living with pain.

CHAPTER TWELVE

IT WAS awful, being back.

Oh, it was nice to see her family again, nice to catch up with everyone and be back in her own flat, for about half a day.

Leah had never been more cold in her life, which seemed strange as the weatherman insisted every evening before she headed for work that it was one of the mildest winters on record, but, permanently frozen, Leah swaddled herself in jumpers and thick woolly stockings. At the end of a long night shift, wrapping a thick scarf around her neck, she pulled out her scrunchy, smiling as Sue, one of her colleagues, came and joined her at the mirror.

'Are you coming to Kathy's leaving do next week?' Sue asked brightly as Leah pulled on her endless layers of clothes. 'The honeymoon's finally over and they're heading back down under!'

'I've been to more of Kathy's leaving dos than I can count,' Leah said, forcing a smile, 'but, then, I guess it's not every day that you emigrate. My name's already on the list.'

Huddling into her seat on the tube, she headed for what she'd once called home, staring blankly ahead like the rest of the passengers, wrapped in her own world as the underground train zipped through the tunnels. At the end of her journey she picked up her bag and trudged the invariably broken escalator before walking the short distance to her flat.

She hated turning the key in the door of her flat, hated walking in, even missed Cole looking at the clock and moaning she was late. There were endless phone calls before she finally made it to bed. Kara, her mother, a couple of aunts all whooping 'Happy birthday' down the phone, but when eleven a.m. came and went, Leah finally gave in and took the phone off the hook. It was midnight in Australia.

If Cole was going to ring, he'd have done so by now.

'Hell, it's as cold as the morgue in here.' Flicking on the lights, Kathy barged in as Leah stood blinking and shivering in her pyjamas. 'And about as lively! Were you still in bed?'

'Well, I did work all night,' Leah moaned, following her through to the lounge. 'We're not all on our honeymoon.'

'And what a honeymoon!' Kathy winked. 'I can't wait to get back to Australia, though. I still don't really feel married—it feels as if it's all a bit of a game. I can't wait to be finally in our own home. Mum said they're going to come out and see us next summer so that makes leaving a bit easier. Anyway, enough about me—you're the birthday girl!'

'Don't,' Leah groaned, taking the parcel Kathy thrust at her and opening it half-heartedly. 'Mum's booked a restaurant for tomorrow. I've got every Jacobs in the phone book coming, I think.'

'And Dale and I.' Kathy grinned. 'It will be a blast.'

'A blast from the past,' Leah sighed. 'Half of these relatives I haven't seen since I was twelve. I don't know why Mum's going to all this fuss—it's only my thirtieth, for goodness' sake.' Her jaw dropped open as the wrapping paper slid off. 'Kathy, this is gorgeous,' Leah gasped, holding up the pale grey woollen dress. 'It must have cost you a fortune.'

'It nearly cost me my sanity,' Kathy sighed coming over and picking up the dress. 'I know how cold you always are but warm and sexy don't exactly equate in my book. Still, this is just divine, isn't it? Go on, then, get dressed—the table's booked for an hour's time.'

'Table?' Leah gave a horrified look. 'Oh, Kathy, no, I really don't want to go out.'

'I don't care what you want,' Kathy insisted. 'You're coming. It's not every day a girl turns thirty, and if I'm giving up a Friday night with my brand-new husband, the least you can do is put on a bit of make-up and a smile.'

'Kathy, I'm really not in the mood.' Leah gave a shrug. 'I want to stay home...'

'In case the phone rings.'

Leah gave an embarrassed nod. 'He knows it's my birthday. I was moaning about turning thirty soon the whole time we were together.'

'If he does ring,' Kathy ventured, 'wouldn't it be better if he got the answering machine, thought you were actually out enjoying yourself rather than picking it up on the second ring and bursting into tears at the sound of his voice?'

'I miss him, Kathy.' Leah's eyes sparkled with tears. 'And the more I think about it, the more I realise that given what had happened it was hardly the right night to pick a row and hope for logical answers. What happened at the train crash—'

'Was awful,' Kathy broke in. 'But for both of you, Leah. You had every right to want to talk about it, every right to draw on Cole for comfort. It's his fault he couldn't give it, not yours for demanding it.

'But if it's any consolation I think you two are made for each other. I'd give anything to see you together, but it has to be right, Leah. Cole has to face up to his issues and he wasn't about to do that with you there. Now, come on,' she said, changing the subject to Leah's dismay, 'we're down to forty-five minutes. Go on,' she shooed, ignoring Leah's protests. 'You've got a lot of work to do, you're going to need every last one of them.'

Only your best friend could get away with being so honest, but as Leah eyed herself in the mirror she knew Kathy was right. The sallow, pinched face that stared back at her seemed a world away from the sun-kissed cheeks of a few short weeks ago. Even her eyes seemed to have paled and her hair fell in a limp, sad mass around her shoulders.

Still, by the time she'd showered and used every trick in the book, even Leah was pretty pleased with the results. Standing back, she admired her reflection in the bedroom mirror, a tiny well of excitement building at the prospect of a long overdue night on the town with her friend.

'I hate to do this.' Not bothering to knock, Kathy came into the bedroom, mobile phone in hand and an apologetic grimace on her face. 'Dale just rang, he's got flu. I know it sounds really wet, but I don't think I should leave him.'

'He's not a two-year-old, Kathy!' Leah grinned, sure her friend would come good, sure that a few months of wedded bliss surely hadn't rendered her quite that pathetic. 'He's a doctor, for heaven's sake, he doesn't need a babysitter.'

'I know.' Kathy shrugged. 'But he sounds really sick. He's asked if I can come home. We could do the restaurant another night,' Kathy suggested. 'It wasn't as if you were that keen anyway.'

Maybe she hadn't been particularly keen but, having gone to the effort, having finally decided to go out, it was a bitter blow when it was swiped away from you. Sinking to the sofa as Kathy left, Leah let out a disappointed sigh, not even bothering to get up when the door knocked almost instantaneously.

Kathy must have forgotten her bag—the intercom hadn't even gone off.

'It's open,' Leah called, swallowing back the tears, not wanting Kathy to see she was upset.

'I could give a lecture here.'

Leah froze, literally froze as the voice that had filled her dreams for the past weeks finally materialised.

'I mean,' Cole said, letting himself in and walking towards her with infuriating stealth, 'if I was the kind of guy who got hung up on that type of thing, now would be the perfect opportunity to warn you of the pitfalls of living in London and leaving your front door wide open.'

The first thing she noticed was his tan and for a second it infuriated her, that he had the gall to look so disgustingly healthy, the gall to walk in here looking so divine when she felt so drab in comparison.

'There is an intercom system.' So ridiculous was her greeting even Leah let out a low laugh as the explanation left her lips. Cole was here, he was really here, and she was talking about security. 'You have to know someone to get past the front door. I thought you were Kathy.'

'I know.'

A flicker of a smile dusted his lips. As for Leah, the penny finally dropped.

'Kathy knew you were coming?' Leah looked up, truly appalled at her friend's lack of honour. Any decent friend would have warned her. It was like the *This is Your Life* cameras turning up with absolutely no forewarning. 'She knew?' Leah checked again.

'Apparently you're not the type of girl who would want to be caught without her mascara on, so she came up with this plan to lure you out for dinner.'

It was easier to focus on the superfluous, easier to talk about the meaningless than to comprehend the truth.

Cole was here, he was really here, and as realisation hit, as truth finally dawned, Leah fell on him, ran to him. Pride, indifference, the million greetings she had rehearsed in her mind didn't merit a thought as he scooped her into his arms, kissed her, condensing four long lonely weeks into one passionate embrace…

'I'm sorry,' he said finally, when he came up for air, 'sorry for all I've put you through. Even though I couldn't see it at the time, I know now that you were right to go,' Cole said softly, as Leah started in confusion, only breathing out when he spoke again. 'Not that I want a repeat, of course.'

Sitting on the sofa, he pulled her onto his knee, wrapping her in his arms, and Leah curled up like a kitten as Cole buried his face in her hair, taking a moment to enjoy the closeness before the inevitable talking started.

'I couldn't believe you just let me go,' Leah admitted. 'I knew it was right to leave and everything, but deep down I was hoping it would serve as a wake-up call, hoping…' She swallowed hard. 'Hoping you'd at least try and stop me. I didn't really want to leave, Cole.'

'But you had to,' he said slowly, and there was no question in his voice, just understanding. 'Fay told me what flight you were on. I drove to the airport and I watched you leave, Leah. I watched you go through the doors and I could see you looking through the crowd, trying to find me, to see if I'd come and stop you…'

'You were there,' Leah gasped as he took her hands.

'Oh, I was there, Leah. And the easiest thing in the world would have been to shout out to you, to beg you to stay, to tell you I'd change.'

'Then why didn't you?'

Cole let out a long sigh. 'How many times a day do we see it in our work, Leah? People swearing they'll change, that this is the last drink, the last hit, the last time they black their wife's eye, the last time she'll let him?'

'Too many.'

'If I was going to promise you that, then it had to mean something. The day you left I went up to Special Care to see the baby.'

'I saw you,' Leah admitted.

'I kidded myself it was just for an update, but the nurses offered to let me hold him.' Lifting her chin, he turned her to face him. 'I was so angry with you, Leah. Till that point I truly thought I was right but, holding that little boy, I realised what I'd lost, realised that it wasn't you I was angry with at all but myself. And...' he swallowed hard and it would have been so easy to jump in and save him the pain, but she held her tongue, knowing this needed to be said '...I was angry with Heather too.'

'For leaving you?'

Cole shook his head. 'She didn't have any choice in that.' He pulled her closer, buried his face in her hair. Resting her head on his chest, she listened as he spoke, listened as he told his awful story because, quite simply, he had to.

'Heather and I had tried for a baby for ages. We were just about to go off and have all the tests when, bingo! Heather didn't want to tell anyone, thought she might somehow jinx the pregnancy, but almost the second she found out she started doing up the spare room. She was so excited, so happy to know she was going to finally be a mother. I had some annual leave due, so we decided on one last romantic holiday before we were laden down with carry cots and nappies. 'We went to Cairns. That's why I ignored you on the plane, that's why I was so rude. The last time I did that journey, I was escorting…'

His voice trailed off as her eyes screwed tightly closed. No wonder he had snubbed her on the plane, no wonder he had asked for his eye shield. Why wouldn't he have wanted to shut out the world, why wouldn't he have wanted to block out the memories when the last time he had travelled that path had been with his dead wife's body?

'It was one of those holidays with all the watersports included, Heather's perfect holiday. She was incredibly fit, loved all that sort of thing. She wanted to go out on a jet-ski. I didn't want to at first, given she was pregnant and all, but Heather just wouldn't let it drop. She insisted she knew exactly what she was doing. The water was like glass it was so smooth. We had a ball, like you do when you're on holiday.'

Leah gave a pensive smile, trying to imagine this difficult man letting down his guard like that and aching for the day she might witness it. But as she felt him stiffen, heard his breath coming shorter, harder, she knew the horrible bit was coming and braced herself just to listen, to not react, but it was hard, so very hard.

'There were some kids on jet-skis, just having a laugh, mucking around, but suddenly they were on top of us. One of them lost control and Heather swerved to avoid him and we both tipped off as they came close.' He was talking in an almost detached mode now, reciting the events like a newsreader. 'It was over in seconds. I came up for air and I honestly thought she'd be waving at me. We had life jackets on, and the water was calm after all, but she was face down, not moving…'

Leah hadn't meant to cry. She'd tried to stay strong but she gave in then, hot, salty tears slipping on to his chest as he spoke, each word an agony in itself.

'She'd broken her neck and that was it. There was nothing, *nothing* I could do. We got her to shore, I gave her CPR, did everything I could…'

'Did you get her back at all?' Leah choked, and felt rather than saw him shake his head.

'She died in my arms on the beach.'

'Oh, Cole.' She didn't even try to be strong, just wept in his arms for all he'd been through, for all he'd suffered. But not only for Cole—for a baby who hadn't stood a chance and for Heather, too, a young woman on the threshold of her dreams who'd lost everything.

'We should have known better,' Cole rasped, and the agony behind his words caught Leah unawares as finally that austere mask slipped, finally he let her in, showed her the true chasm of his despair. 'What the hell was Heather doing on a jet-ski when she was four months pregnant, how irresponsible was that? And what the hell was I doing, letting her go on?'

'It's called living, Cole,' Leah said gently, lifting her head and watching him as she spoke, sad, so sad for all he'd been through but so very proud of him for finally sharing. 'We make choices every day, some good, some bad. With hindsight you might have done things differently, but neither of you deserved what happened. It was an accident.'

'I know,' Cole admitted. 'I know that now, but it's taken a long time. When I was holding the baby the dad came in and we spoke for a while, and I could hear myself in every word he said. ''What the hell was she doing, getting a train? She should have been at home, she was a week overdue, for goodness' sake.'' The same pointless arguments you berate yourself with when you've lost someone, the same futile bargaining you put yourself through as you re-live the day it all ended, trying to work out how it could have been done differently. Listening to the baby's dad, I realised it could just as well have been me talking.

'I love you, Leah.' His eyes raked hers and she didn't even have to say it back, it was all there in her eyes. 'I think I loved you the first day I met you and certainly by the second day.'

'I loved you then, too.'

'We'd have ended up in bed, you know.' He grinned and it was so nice to see him smile, such a relief to see the light back in his eyes, that Leah smiled too.

'You'd have thought I was cheap. I'd have proba-bly had a lecture the following morning on the perils of casual sex!'

'Probably.' Cole grinned. 'But what I'm trying to say, and even though it's not much of a defence it's all I've got, is that though we barely knew each other I already had feelings for you, Leah. And no matter how you play it down, the fact is you nearly died in my arms that night.'

Her heart stilled for a moment. Seeing that first night from Cole's perspective, she truly registered his fear.

'I couldn't face it happening again. I couldn't bear to find you only to lose you, but I lost you anyway,' Cole rasped. 'I was so busy trying to hold onto you that I pushed you away.'

'Cole, it wasn't your over-protectiveness that pushed me away. I could deal with that and I knew you were trying. It was you who encouraged me to go back to nursing, you who encouraged me to go on nights—it was your emotional shutdown I couldn't take.

'Have you seen someone?'

'No.' Cole gave a slight grimace. 'Unless you count daily phone calls from Kathy, telling me what an idiot I am, telling me to buck up and do something.'

'Kathy's been ringing you?'

'Ringing me?' Cole gave her an exasperated look. 'I think her phone must be on permanent redial. I swear if I hadn't flown in last week she'd have come and got me herself.'

'Last week?' Leah stared at him bemused. 'You've been here all this time...' The thought that he'd been in the same country and hadn't even thought to look her up, the knowledge he had been so close and hadn't thought to contact her, was almost too much to comprehend.

'You were working,' Cole said patiently, 'which,

according to Kathy, meant the flat would look like a bomb and the inhabitant something similar.' He stared at her non-comprehending face. 'According to your friend, girls like to look their best when an unexpected guest drops by.'

Truth, however farfetched, however impossible, was starting to dawn. 'This was all a set-up.'

'She's probably outside with a glass against the wall.' Cole grinned. 'I chose the dress…' he gave her a slow smile '…but I take no responsibility for the restaurant tomorrow.'

He'd really got her confused now.

'Tomorrow night.' Cole smiled. 'Your mum just went off, ringing up people, booking bands and balloons.'

'Mum and Dad know that you're here?'

Cole nodded. 'Call me old-fashioned but I wanted to do things properly. I asked their permission.'

'For what?'

It was a stupid question when surely there could only be one answer, but after so much pain, so much agony elation seemed to be hanging around reluctantly outside the door, terrified it might be shooed away, terrified it might somehow have got things wrong. But a very nice aquamarine bag was heading its way into her hands. It was topped with a white bow and unless Leah was very much mistaken she could feel the weight of something nestled at the bottom.

'Happy birthday,' Cole said gruffly, handing her a card, which Leah promptly ignored. 'You're supposed to read the card first,' Cole nudged as Leah completely ignored him, tearing at the bow with shaking fingers. 'Leah.' Looking up, she took the card with a reluctant sigh, politely opening the envelope then frowning as a ticket fell into her lap.

'What's this?' She read it for a moment, the ring almost forgotten as she read the voucher slowly before turning to him, an incredulous tinge to her voice. 'You've paid for me to take a parachute jump?'

'Two, actually. One in Australia, one in England. It's up to you, Leah.' For a second she could have sworn he looked nervous. 'If you can't leave I understand…'

'You'd live here?' Leah gasped. 'You'd give up your job…'

'In a heartbeat,' Cole said, 'if it meant keeping you.'

'You don't have to do that,' Leah gulped. 'I'll clean the windows in Emergency if it means I can be with you. It was never about the job, Cole. I just couldn't give everything up if I didn't have all of you.' Staring down at the tickets, a tiny frown puckered her brow. 'But a parachute jump! Why on earth…?'

'I wanted to show you how much I'm trying, that I'm not going to hold you back…'

'Cole, you've never held me back. The only person you've held back is yourself.' She let out a low laugh. 'It's a wonderful thought, but I haven't got some sort of death wish—the last thing I want to do is jump out of a plane. Anyway…' she gave him a slow smile '…it wouldn't be very responsible.'

'Don't.' Shaking his head, Cole put up his hand. 'I am trying, Leah. Don't throw what I said back at me.'

'I'm not,' Leah said softly, and this time she looked nervous, this time it was she who couldn't quite meet his eyes. 'It's a wonderful gift and I know how hard it would have been for you to choose it, but...'

Catching his eyes, so infinitely divine were they, so blazing with love and adoration, even a Tiffany ring nestled in its bag couldn't drag her away. 'What I'm trying to say, Cole, is that I know how hard it would have been for you to choose this for me, and as much as the thought truly terrifies me, under any other circumstances I'd be thrilled to accept.' She swallowed hard, watching as a frown creased his brow, knowing he was waiting for an explanation and wondering just how best to give it. 'You see, jumping out of a plane wouldn't be very responsible for a woman in my condition.'

For an age he didn't say anything, just stared back at her, the silence growing around them until finally Leah rushed to fill it. 'I know it's not ideal timing. I didn't mean for it to happen, it just did...'

'How long...?'

'Eight weeks.' Leah gulped as Cole stared back at her.

'You've known for eight weeks?' He gasped, and Leah quickly shook her head.

'I'm eight weeks pregnant.' Still his eyes didn't give a clue. 'Which means I was pregnant when I abseiled down the embankment.'

'You didn't know, though,' Cole said gently, a tiny

smile inching its way along his lips. 'And it certainly doesn't seem to have done any harm.'

'But I had all those tests for my chest injury,' Leah gulped. 'I've been going through hell wondering if it could have caused any damage. I rang Dr Crean's office when I found out.' She saw the start in his eyes and carried on talking quickly. 'But it wouldn't have done any harm either. I didn't have a chest X-ray or anything.' She was gabbling now, trying to pour out a million jumbled emotions, to condense them into one succinct sentence. 'I had a scan a couple of days ago and the radiographer says that everything looks perfect.'

'Everything is perfect.' Cole's strong words stilled her momentarily, quelled her fears, made the world good and safe. 'We're going to have a wonderfully healthy baby and put all the nightmares behind us now, Leah.'

'You're not upset?' she checked, and Cole half laughed as he shook his head, his hand incredulously exploring the flat plane of her stomach.

'I couldn't be less upset,' he whispered in that low sexy drawl that had her toes curling.

'This isn't going to undo all the work you've done?' Leah said. 'I mean, you're not suddenly going to demand I take vitamins and don't lift a single cup...'

'Probably.' Cole laughed. 'But reel me in when I go too far.'

His kiss sealed it then, sealed the love that had simmered for so long unattended, sealed the passion and the pain that had held them together and torn them apart.

'Cole,' Leah squeaked, pushing him away, grinning at the shock on his face at her abrupt withdrawal. 'Isn't there something you've forgotten? I mean, kissing you is divine and everything, but it is my birthday.' She gestured frantically at the little bag. 'Isn't there something you wanted to ask me?'

'You want your keyring now?' Cole frowned, handing her the bag.

'It's a keyring?'

'With a key on it.' Cole smiled softly. 'For when you're ready to come home.'

Which was a lovely gesture and everything, but Leah struggled to keep the disappointment from her face as she pulled off the bow and peered in the bag.

Oh, she knew a ring didn't matter, that there was plenty of time for all that later, that the fact Cole was here was more than enough, but feeling the shape of a key through the pouch she bit back a little sigh.

'Aren't you going to open it?'

'Later.' Leah smiled, turning back to kiss him, embarrassed at her own presumption and determined not to show it. 'Now, where were we?'

'You're a lousy actress,' Cole said, taking the pouch from her lap and prising it open. 'One key,' he said softly, holding it up, but Leah wasn't looking. What was holding her attention was the other object Cole was pulling out of the pouch. 'And one ring,' he added, holding up a band of gold with a diamond that could almost have qualified for its own donkey, given the amount of carats involved.

'Is this what you were hoping for?' Cole asked, slipping the ring on *that* finger. The catch in his voice told Leah he was as moved as her, told Leah that despite the little game he was taking this moment just as seriously as her.

'It's everything I hoped for, Cole,' she whispered.

Oh, it was a beautiful ring, everything a girl could wish for and all that, but after a moment's gazing she stared up into something infinitely more beautiful and precious: the look of love from her future husband.

EPILOGUE

'GIVE your crazy mummy a kiss and tell her we'll see her soon.'

Leah stood, teeth chattering in her green overalls, fiddling with the straps on her hard hat as Cole looked on, a smile on his face as for the hundredth time she changed her mind.

'I don't want to do this, Cole.'

'Yes, you do,' he said patiently. 'It's all you've talked about for weeks.'

'No, I don't,' Leah insisted. Taking Gemma from Cole, she held her little girl close, breathing in the sweet baby smell, kissing the fat little hands jabbing at her face. 'It was all very well doing these adventure sports when I was backpacking—I was single then,' Leah pointed out. 'And if the truth be known, I hated doing them. That bungy-jump was the most frightening thing I've ever done.'

'But you're glad you did it,' Cole reminded her as Leah pulled Gemma even closer. 'The picture's got pride of place in the living room—you can't wait for people to notice it so it can give you an excuse to talk about it. And this will be the same. I've got the camera ready, Kathy's taking the video.'

'I'm a wife and mother now, and jumping out of a plane isn't exactly the most responsible thing to do.'

'Leah.' Prising Gemma out of her arms, Cole

kissed her chattering lips. 'They're waiting for you. If you don't go now, the plane will leave without you.'

'I don't care,' Leah insisted, but as Cole took her arm and walked her over she didn't put up too much resistance.

'It's last-minute nerves,' Cole insisted. 'And if you don't do it, not only will you regret it for ever but you'll bend my ear about the fact all the way back to Melbourne. And then your birthday dinner's going to be a complete non-starter, with you feeling sorry for yourself.

'Come on, Leah,' he said with a smile, nodding to the waiting team who were looking over impatiently. 'It's your thirty-first birthday today. You said yourself you wanted to do something special. Now give Gemma a quick kiss and go.'

Kissing her daughter's smiling, innocent face, Leah turned her face to Cole, closing her eyes as his strong mouth quelled her pale, quivering lips.

'Go!' he said again as Leah stalled at the final hurdle. 'We'll be right here waiting for you.'

This made even childbirth look easy, Leah thought as she sat on the hard bench in the plane, staring fixedly ahead, not even smiling at her fellow daredevils.

It was all very well for Cole to tell her she could do it, Leah thundered internally as she stood, reluctantly moving up the line, wincing every time the light changed from red to green and another idiot jumped. Cole thought he was doing her a favour, showing her he had changed, but that was all behind them now. They'd dealt with all that months ago and Cole had nothing more to prove.

She didn't need to do this!

The sensible thing to do would be to turn back now. Cole would understand—he probably didn't want her to jump anyway.

But suddenly it was *her* light turning green, the instructor giving her a thumbs-up. And even before a thought pattern emerged, even before she could register her protest, she was nodding, holding her breath and jumping, falling out of the plane with a delicious, exhilarating scream, freefalling through the air with a heady sense of freedom. As she pulled her ripcord, as the chute dragged her upwards, caught her fall, Leah knew what it felt like to be on the top of the world.

The view was amazing. She could see for miles and miles, the endless roads, the rivers running dry, the clear blue sky and the parched yellow grass. But best of all, as she drifted down she could see Cole waving frantically, holding onto Gemma just as he had promised he would be…

Bravely waiting for Leah to come back to him.

HARLEQUIN®
INTRIGUE®

WE'LL LEAVE YOU BREATHLESS!

If you've been looking for thrilling tales of
contemporary passion and sensuous love stories
with taut, edge-of-the-seat suspense—then
you'll love Harlequin Intrigue!

Every month, you'll meet six new heroes
who are guaranteed to make your spine tingle
and your pulse pound. With them you'll enter
into the exciting world of Harlequin Intrigue—
where your life is on the line
and so is your heart!

THAT'S INTRIGUE—
ROMANTIC SUSPENSE
AT ITS BEST!

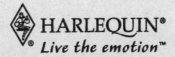

HARLEQUIN®
Live the emotion™

passionate powerful provocative love stories

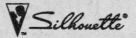

**Silhouette Desire delivers
strong heroes, spirited heroines
and compelling love stories.**

Desire features your favorite authors,
including

Annette Broadrick,
Ann Major,
Anne McAllister
and Cait London.

**Passionate, powerful and provocative
romances *guaranteed!***

For superlative authors, sensual stories
and sexy heroes, choose Silhouette Desire.

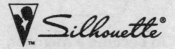

passionate powerful provocative love stories

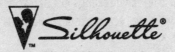